Journe[illegible] the Unified Field

Journey Through the Unified Field

Col. Cassie B. Barlow, USAF (ret)
and Sue Hill Norrod

Foreword by Amanda Wright Lane
Illustrations by Amy Gantt

PELICAN PUBLISHING COMPANY
GRETNA 2019

Library of Congress Cataloging-in-Publication Data

Names: Barlow, Cassie B., author. | Norrod, Sue Hill, author. | Gantt, Amy, illustrator.
Title: Journey through the unified field / by Col. Cassie B. Barlow, USAF (ret), and Sue Hill Norrod ; foreword by Amanda Wright Lane ; illustrated by Amy Gantt.
Description: Gretna : Pelican Publishing Company, 2019. | Summary: Emma's summer at her grandfather's STEM school takes an interesting turn when she uses virtual reality to help save her pilot father from imprisonment in Somalia.
Identifiers: LCCN 2019000296| ISBN 9781455624782 (pbk. : alk. paper) | ISBN 9781455624799 (ebook)
Subjects: | CYAC: Summer schools—Fiction. | Schools—Fiction. | Virtual reality—Fiction. | Adventure and adventurers—Fiction.
Classification: LCC PZ7.1.B37079 Jo 2019 | DDC [Fic]—dc23 LC record available at https://lccn.loc.gov/2019000296

Printed in the United States of America
Published by Pelican Publishing Company, Inc.
1000 Burmaster Street, Gretna, Louisiana 70053
www.pelicanpub.com

I would like to dedicate this book to all the men and women who have chosen the most noble profession in the world—teacher! They give of their time and treasure for the young people in their communities. They are all focused on making the world a better place and on building the next generation. This is *the most important profession in our country, and we need to continue to attract the best and brightest to be teachers. Thanks Mom and Dad for giving your life to the betterment of others!*

—Col. Cassie B. Barlow, USAF (ret)

I would like to dedicate this book to all of the students who don't think that they are very good at science. I remember such feelings when I was a young middle school student interested in art. I hope that by reading this book you will begin to see how your interests fit into the Grand Unified Theory. Most of all, I hope you discover and want to learn more about its creation and what holds it all together!

—Sue Hill Norrod

Contents

Foreword

Bishop Milton Wright—the father of Orville, Wilbur, Katharine, and four other Wright siblings—experienced flight only one time in his life, on a beautiful day in May in the early 1900s. As the flying machine piloted by his son gained altitude over Huffman Prairie outside of Dayton, Ohio, the eighty-year-old patriarch shouted, "Higher, Orville, higher!"

Col. Cassie Barlow and Sue Norrod's latest work, *Journey Through the Unified Field*, is also about the exhilaration of climbing higher and challenging the norm. Through the life experiences of their young, middle school heroine, Emma, the authors elevate values we revere as Americans and ask us to embrace some changing ones.

Emma is a young lady who is feeling a little lost. She is part of a loving family, and her father serves in the US Air Force in the Middle East. Emma struggles with worry, as she understands her dad's assignments are dangerous. At home in Dayton, Emma's mother and grandfather look for a way to give Emma an "assignment" as well, only this one challenges her intellect. Emma is asked to assist at a summer camp that emphasizes the disciplines of STEAM (science, technology, engineering, the arts, and mathematics) learning. While Emma is very unsure about her own aptitude for these lessons, she not only soars but also makes a whole new discovery in, shall we say, a very interesting classroom.

Barlow and Norrod's approach weaves together early history lessons from the birthplace of aviation—Dayton,

Ohio—with the ever-changing aerospace future, led by our US military. It is also, however, a story about the dawn of young Emma's journey toward a future that she could never have imagined as a young lady in the early 1900s. But today? . . . higher, Emma, higher!

Amanda Wright Lane
Great-grandniece of Orville and Wilbur Wright
Trustee for the Wright Family Foundation of the Dayton Foundation

Acknowledgments

This book has been a journey into many areas beyond our expertise. We are thankful for the friends who edited chapters and for the experts who made our cybersecurity chapters and Navy SEAL rescue as accurate as possible for this audience. We would like to acknowledge all who have helped make this book possible, starting with a special thanks to our contributing chapter writers:

Fredrick F. Hall (Courtesy Mr. Hall.)

Fredrick F. "Frank" Hall retired from the US Army and is currently a federal civil servant. He helped to explain the dangers and importance of cybersecurity in chapter 6 and explained realistic avoidance cybermaneuvers in chapter 13. He is an information technology professional. In his off time, Fredrick is a CyberPatriot coach in the San Antonio area and is also a member of the Texas Computer Science Task Force for the Center for STEM Education at the University of Texas at Austin College of Education. He is a member of the Information Technology Cluster Advisory Council for the Texas Education Agency. He also serves as a Boy Scouts of America merit badge counselor for digital technology and a cybersafety instructor.

Richard "Rick" Kaiser, BMCM SEAL (ret), is the executive director of the National Navy SEAL Museum in Fort

Rick Kaiser (Courtesy Mr. Kaiser.)

Pierce, Florida. He joined the US Navy at age seventeen and was assigned to East Coast SEAL Teams in 1980. Rick served from 1985 to 1993, acting as lead diver, breacher, and sniper. In 1993, Rick received the Silver Star for his actions during the Battle of Mogadishu (or Black Hawk Down). Rick made numerous deployments to Bosnia until his retirement from active duty in August 2000, after twenty-two years of service. Rick was rehired after 9/11 and, from 2001 to 2012, oversaw and managed numerous combat deployments of SEALs to many other locations around the world.

Robin Brown, language arts teacher, proofread and made suggestions in several chapters.

Laura Funderburg, of Funderburg Farms in Yellow Springs, Ohio, provided a tour, which included an introduction to her beautiful horses.

Major Tom Gills (ret) is a retired USAF Catholic chaplain. Chaplain Gills advised on the Missing in Action notification of the family in chapter 7.

Jason Sopko, an electrical engineer and patent lawyer for the United States Air Force, advised on the discussion of the electromagnetic spectrum in chapter 2.

Jonathan Miller, Wright-Patterson Air Force Base engineer, provided scientific explanations during the initial stages of writing the book.

Sherrie Miller proofread and made editing suggestions to early drafts of the book.

Cynthia Williams edited the final manuscript to ensure the book was prepared for publishing.

Xenia Public Schools, in Xenia, OH, provided curriculum books that helped with ideas regarding physical science standards.

1

Summer STEAM

Emma awoke to the light streaming through the blinds in her bedroom window. The faint sound of frying bacon, along with her little brother Max's chatter, came drifting up the stairs into her room. Normally, the first day of summer break would be a happy celebration for the Harris family of four, but Emma's mood was tempered with heaviness. Dad was on a long-overdue deployment to Africa with the United States Air Force. She missed him terribly. She felt as though nothing was going well in her life right now.

She sat up on the edge of her bed and stretched as she looked at familiar drawings on her sky-blue wall. She loved to draw. It had been a good way for her to release the tension and emotions that arose since her family moved all the way from Arizona to Wright-Patterson Air Force Base in Ohio. She particularly loved to draw horses. Her sketchbook was full of them. She longed to be in Arizona again, where she could go over to her best friend McKayla's house on Saturdays to groom and feed McKayla's horse named Sugar. She loved to rub Sugar's velvety soft nose and scratch him between the eyes after giving him an apple, which was his favorite treat. McKayla had been giving her a few lessons on how to put on a saddle and ride properly. That all came to an abrupt end when her father was transferred to Ohio. She and McKayla stayed in contact every day, but it wasn't the same. The thought of starting the fifth grade in a new city, without McKayla, was dismal. Now cut off from her dad because of his sensitive mission and location, she felt as if everything was suddenly wrong in her life.

She picked up her drawing pad and pencils from her dresser and put them away. "At least I can draw horses and hang them up on my wall," she said despondently. Dad had often told her that she must have gotten her talent from Grandma Harris. Grandma was an artist and loved to draw and use color in any medium. Dad often joked that when Grandma and Grandpa got married, they completed the electromagnetic spectrum. Emma was never quite sure what he meant by that, but she was glad to think she inherited something special from the Harris genes. For generations, the Harrises had been inventors, scientists, and mathematicians, and now at least, it seemed she might have inherited one trait from that gene pool. She certainly didn't think she had inherited the intelligence of her dad and grandfather. They were experts in their fields and the smartest men Emma had ever known. She struggled to understand science and math, which just seemed boring and monotonous to her.

She put on her robe and slippers and glanced in the mirror at her tussled brown hair. She sighed and said, "I'm so glad it is summer break!"

Heading downstairs to join her mother and brother, Max, in the kitchen, her thoughts wandered to images of African savannas that she had recently seen on TV. She wondered what her father was doing. She knew he had an important job. He operated and interpreted data from surveillance unmanned aerial vehicles (UAVs) in Mogadishu, Somalia. His US Air Force unit also delivered food supplies to the people displaced by the civil war. Dad had told them in his last video chat that he was appalled at the way the warlords, or tribal leaders, would steal the food and supplies and sell them on the black market while their own people were starving. His drone surveillance could count the stockpiles and keep track of trucks that might drive in and out of the area. He told them that the sensors on the drone could even see at night, in case the warlords tried to sneak out the supplies under the cover of darkness. Mom worried about his safety because the tribal leaders knew where the UAVs were flying from. She was afraid Dad and his unit would be attacked in retaliation against their interference into the warlords' operations. Dad always kept his conversations light and insisted that he and his unit always stayed one step ahead of the "bad guys." Mom would always try to be brave and smile back at him, so he wouldn't worry about things at home. But Emma knew how she really felt. Several times, late at night, when she had a difficult time falling asleep, she could hear soft crying coming from her mother's room. She wanted to comfort her mother so badly but didn't know what to do. During those moments, she would roll over, squeeze her eyes shut, and pray that it would all be over soon and Dad would be able to come back home.

Emma didn't cry often, but she just couldn't shake a terrible, sinking feeling of experiencing a loss in her life. She missed flying radio-controlled planes, called RCs, with her dad on Saturday mornings at the RC field near their home. She had enjoyed doing that here in Ohio, and it took the place of visiting McKayla and Sugar. Dad would let her fly the plane while he was attached to her controller by a cord using a Buddy Box. A Buddy Box allows a beginner to fly the airplane unhindered by the instructor unless they lose control or panic. At that point, the instructor could release the switch and have control back immediately. Dad told her that was the safest way to learn. He carefully followed all the local ordinances on where to fly RCs safely and how to teach a beginner.

When she did have control, Emma imagined that the plane was an exquisite flying white horse. She could make the plane roll and perform all the split-s maneuvers her dad loved to show her. She was delighted by the whirl of the battery-powered propellers as the plane would fly overhead. Her father was an expert. He could make it climb and dive and crab into the wind, even when the wind was too strong for most experienced pilots to maneuver safely.

She admired him so much. He had always worked in the sensor department of every air base where he was assigned. However, with their recent move to Wright-Patterson Air Force Base, he had been promoted to lead UAV engineer in the Sensors Directorate at the Air Force Research Laboratory. It seemed Dad could fix anything electronic. She hoped that she had inherited some of his "tinkering" skills. She was getting pretty good at charging the batteries for the plane and understanding how signals were intercepted by sensors on the plane. She didn't yet feel confident enough to try to fly without her dad being attached to her controller through the Buddy Box.

Emma brushed aside her thoughts, and with a deep sigh, she walked down the steps and into the kitchen, where her younger brother, Max, was sitting at the table drinking milk and eating waffles and bacon. He looked small in the faded Thunderbirds T-shirt Dad had bought for him last year at the air show. It was a size too big, but he wore it every chance he could get.

"Hi," he said cheerfully. "Today, we're going to the National Museum of the United States Air Force, and then we're going to meet Grandpa at his school!"

Emma's mother turned from the stove and smiled as she said, "Would you like some waffles?"

"Yes, they smell wonderful," she replied. She loved her mother's homemade waffles. They were so light and fluffy. As she took her first delicious bite, Emma savored the Ohio maple syrup that had been a housewarming gift from Grandpa. Her mother sat down across from her with a gleam in her eyes.

"Emma, I've decided to take Grandpa up on his job offer to help out at the STEAM summer camp for six weeks. He said that you could be a paid teacher's aide. Meanwhile, Max could attend the camp with the first-grade kids. Wouldn't it be wonderful to all be together? Max could go on the field trips and play with other kids his age, and we would be right upstairs if he needed us. What do you think?"

Emma looked up from her waffles, absorbed in thought. "Do you think I could earn enough money to take horseback-riding lessons?"

"Yes, you would make more than enough, and we could spend quality time with Grandpa and help him with his summer camp."

"Okay," smiled Emma, "what are the ages of the kids you're working with?"

"I will be assigned to the fifth- and sixth-grade students," her mother replied.

"But don't you think it will be a little weird to have a

fifth-grade girl working as a teacher's aide to fifth and sixth graders?" Emma asked between bites.

"No," Mom replied. "They will probably feel more comfortable around you and be willing to ask for help. You will be perfect."

"But I'm not very good at science and math," Emma said in a discouraged tone. "How can I help them when I squeaked through math and science with a C plus?"

"Don't worry, Emma," Mom replied. "They are learning, just like you. A lot of things are new and different at your grade level. I know it is tempting to give up, but if you push through and keep moving forward, you will succeed. Someday, it will all make sense, and you might even use your knowledge to solve problems or invent new things, like your dad and grandpa do. Remember, they too were beginners once.

"Besides, Grandpa said he's going to help you, and you couldn't have a better teacher than your grandpa! I have a feeling that you will come out of this with a new appreciation for math and science. Who knows? You might even decide that you like it," she smiled.

Emma took a sip of milk and mused about the opportunity to spend time with Grandpa. She had never lived near him until they moved to Ohio. Her parents had said he and Grandma visited them in Germany when she was born, and they visited many times when Emma's father was stationed in Arizona. After Grandma died, Grandpa seemed to pour more of himself into his work and didn't make the trip out to visit as much.

It dawned on Emma that she didn't know much about him, other than that he was a respected engineer who had worked on top-secret programs for the government. Dad once told her Grandpa worked for the Department of Defense on a "Black Program," which meant it was highly secretive and very few knew about it. She sort of imagined him as a secret agent living undercover and working for the military. Maybe he just posed as a retired school administrator to protect his identity. Grandpa had traveled a lot to Washington, DC, and California before he retired last year.

Dad said he thought Grandpa started the STEAM Academy here in Dayton, Ohio, to keep himself busy and to have an outlet for his creative energy. Grandpa would often say, "The future lies with all of our youth, not just with those who have the opportunity to attend better schools." Dad said that was likely why Grandpa wanted to spend his retirement creating a school that would inspire young students at a critical time in their lives.

Grandpa worked hard to receive a grant from the government so he could lease a closed school that was designated to be torn down. He renamed it the STEAM Academy. Once the STEAM Academy got off the ground, concerned citizens and philanthropists joined with Grandpa to start a foundation to keep it going. The STEAM Academy was beginning to get national attention.

Emma rinsed off her dishes, placed them in the dishwasher, and went upstairs to brush her teeth. She knew that this summer camp would help all of them stay busy and keep their minds off of Dad. Getting to know Grandpa a little better and saving up for horseback-riding lessons might make for a fun summer after all.

2

The Stone Castle

"It's a castle," Max exclaimed, looking through the car window as his mom drove up to the STEAM Academy's parking lot. The structure stood four stories tall and was completely made of stone.

"Wow," Emma said in a low voice, "it looks like something out of a storybook."

They parked the car, got out, walked to the front of the building, and stopped. They all looked up at the beautiful architecture. The concrete entrance steps led up to five archways under a covered patio. It almost looked like a church, with its steepled roof, spires, and tall, pointed bell tower. "I can't believe that this was actually going to be torn down," Emma's mother said slowly. "It is such a beautiful old building. Grandpa said it was over one hundred years old and was once Steele High School, built in 1898. The city turned it into a community center after the First World War, and it was scheduled to be torn down. I think he spent most of his grant money fixing it up for his classes."

To the left of the entrance steps stood a large bronze statue of a lion. "Look at the lion," Emma said. "It's amazing. Did it come with the school?" She walked over and touched the six-foot-long bronze sculpture. She could barely reach the bottom of its paw. It stood on a podium and looked intently over their heads and into the distance, over all those entering the building. It was so majestic with the afternoon sun gleaming off the metal. Emma walked around to the front of the statue and gazed into its face. For a moment, she felt transformed into the character Susan from the book *The Lion, the Witch, and the Wardrobe,* written by C. S. Lewis. She felt as if she were looking into the eyes of Aslan the Lion from that famous story. She looked away as Max and her mother walked up to the large, glass door and said softly to herself, "I wonder if there is a magical wardrobe in here somewhere."

"C'mon, Emma," said Max as he eagerly followed their mother across the portico to the front door. Mom leaned on the handle of the door, which opened into the main lobby. Emma saw a young man sitting behind a long, wooden desk near the back of the lobby. At the sound of their entrance, he looked up from his reading and welcomed them in a friendly voice.

"Hello, you must be Dr. Harris's family! Welcome to STEAM!" He walked toward them, gently shook her mother's hand, and smiled at Max and Emma. "Dr. Harris has been delayed in a meeting downtown, and he asked me to meet you and show you around until he gets here. Have you ever been inside the school before?"

"No," they all said in unison, smiling.

"It is certainly larger and grander than I had expected," Mom said.

"Well, let me show you around. Oh, my name is Ryan, and I am a graduate student writing a thesis about STEAM education. I have been working with Dr. Harris on aligning his experiments with fifth-grade educational science standards."

"I'm Sarah Harris, and this is my daughter, Emma, and my son, Max."

He looked down at Max and asked, "How old are you?"

"I'm six, and I'm going to start first grade this year," Max replied.

"Well, then, we simply must see the lower level hallway first," Ryan grinned. They followed him as he led them to double doors at the rear of the lobby, where he scanned his name badge over a sensor by the door. They heard a click, and Ryan pushed open the door, which revealed a long hallway with classrooms. The tile was multicolored, and each door was painted with different primary colors. There were streamers hanging from the ceiling and what looked like, to Emma, a stuffed fish made of tissue paper hanging down between the streamers. "Pre-K through fourth is on this level," Ryan said. "Every week, we have a different theme, and this week, the students will be studying different ecosystems around the world. Have you ever made a robotic alligator and programmed its mouth to open and shut?" he asked Max.

"I've played with the small plastic bricks, but I've never made a robot before," replied Max.

"Well, every day you will explore a different ecosystem through robotics, art, stories, and games. On Fridays, you will go on a field trip with your class on a bus! This Friday, the students are going to a park, where park rangers will wade through creeks with your class and answer all your questions," said Ryan.

Max's eyes got wide, and he looked at his mom and squealed, "This is going to be fun!"

"We even have a gym on this level for you to play in and a lunchroom just for your age group," Ryan smiled. "Now, let's go upstairs, and I'll show you the rest of the school."

They walked through the lobby to the front of the building and began to climb a large, wooden staircase to the right. Emma looked at the intricate carved handrails, which were lighter in color on the top, where the students had run their hands over them through the years.

"This stairwell is beautiful," her mother said. "I love the wooden-paneled walls and the marble steps." At the top of the stairs, Ryan opened the second-floor doors and allowed them to look down the hallway.

"This floor is used primarily for lectures, tutoring, and teacher workshops. We train teachers to teach science standards using the hands-on experiments we have set up. They can earn continuing education units to renew their teaching licenses. It is a win-win scenario for us because through their teachers, we can reach all the students who didn't have a chance to come to the STEAM Academy.

"We also have a college prep class to allow high school students to study for their ACT and SAT exams. Dr. Harris has helped many students get into colleges that they once thought were out of their reach. He has many volunteer teachers who help students with study skills and preparation. On the other end of this floor is a lunchroom for the middle school and a band room, where the STEAM Band practices for summer performances around the Dayton area." Ryan shut the door, and they turned to climb the stairs again.

Mrs. Harris asked, "Can you tell us a little about the building's history?"

"Well, it was built in 1898, and I think the most amazing

fact that not many people know is that Katharine Wright, the sister of Wilbur and Orville Wright, once taught Latin and English here. In fact, her classroom was on the third floor, down at the far end, and overlooks the Great Miami River."

"Wow!" exclaimed Emma, who had quietly been taking in the tour. "Did the Wright brothers ever go here?"

"No," replied Ryan, "neither of them finished high school. In fact, Katharine finished college during a time that not many women even worked outside of the home. She was very active in helping women get the right to vote. She was an excellent teacher and was often heard telling her students to be sure to take the trolley out to Huffman Prairie on the weekend to see her brothers' flying machine."

"Oh, that's a great story," said Mom. "I wonder how many students who didn't go wish they had taken her up on the suggestion to see them fly."

As they climbed the stairs to the third floor, Emma asked, "What about the lion? Has he always been here?"

"The lion's name is Leo. He was dedicated on December 11, 1909. The students had a nickel drive and collected three hundred dollars in nickels to pay for him to be cast and mounted outside their school. I don't think you could cast a lion in bronze today for three hundred dollars in nickels. Do you?

"Now, this is where you both will be working this summer," Ryan said as they reached the top of the steps. He scanned his ID badge and pushed open the third-floor doors. The coolness of the air-conditioning was welcoming to Emma after climbing the flight of stairs.

"Let me switch on the lights, so you can experience the full effect," he added. Suddenly, the long hallway came alive with color, lights, and images of rockets, sculptures, and science equipment lining the walls. Emma couldn't help but be amazed at the brilliantly lit marquee lights shaped in the form of a letter over each door. As she looked down the hallway, she saw they spelled out S-T-E-A-M. Ryan walked to the entrance of the room with the S over the top of the door.

"This is where you and Emma will be working. It is the Science Lab," he said to Emma's mother. They walked inside a room bright from the windows on one side. It was a long room with two rows of tables. Each section had different colored tables in the three sections that made up the laboratory. Ryan pointed out the different colors and explained that each section focused on different hands-on activities to teach specific fifth-grade science standards.

"What are these?" asked Max as he ran over to the window and touched a wooden catapult.

"Those are called trebuchets," Ryan said. He walked over to the window, picked one up, and set it on the table in front of Max. "This helps to teach the concept of mass, force, and distance, which is part of the fifth-grade physical science lesson. Let's point it at the wall this way, and I want you to load it up with one of the clay balls in the caddy." Max put the clay ball in the sling, and Ryan added the weight. Then Ryan told him to pull the wooden dowel rod in the front. Immediately, the sling swung around and released the clay ball, and it was tossed into the wall. Max squealed with excitement and wanted to do it again. This time, he tried a lighter clay mass, and Ryan placed a heavier weight, which sent the ball flying even faster. It hit the wall with a solid thud.

Everyone laughed at the sound as Max ran to pick up the clay ball and held it up for all to see. "Look at how much it flattened the ball," he exclaimed as he handed it to Ryan. "That was amazing!"

"We use these trebuchets to teach that the amount of

change in the movement of an object is based on the mass of the object and the amount of force exerted. In this case, the clay ball represents the mass, and the force exerted depends on the weight applied in the box. The students experiment with different masses and different weights and record which combinations create the greatest distance or "change in movement" from where the ball is thrown." Ryan explained. "Those are the technical reasons behind the principle of this science standard, but actually, the students learn it easily by being given time to play and experiment and record their observations as a group," he smiled.

"This is why I came here this summer. I want to help create lessons for teachers that make learning fun. I was one of those kids who learned tactually. I had to touch and manipulate something to really learn it. I couldn't just take notes and memorize facts," Ryan said as he looked at Mom.

"I have found that there are many kids who learn the way I did. I am making it my life's mission to help them to progress and learn in their styles until they can learn adaptation skills as they get older. This is the basis of the thesis I am writing this summer," he explained.

"Albert Einstein was like this when he was younger. He had a passion for moving parts and puzzles and once built a card tower that was fourteen stories tall. He was all about hands-on. He visualized experiments in his mind and loved to tinker. It was only after imagining events happening in time and space that he put them down on paper. Then they would become his words and equations.

"Dr. Harris and I want to try to capture those kinds of students and steer them into the possibility of a science career. They are the most at risk to be turned off by the routine of the day-to-day school curriculum and sometimes turn away from science altogether."

Emma listened intently to Ryan's passionate views on education. She found his ideas interesting. "Who knows?" she thought. "Maybe I am really good at science deep down." She could really relate to Einstein in that school was mundane and not interesting to her also. She smiled at the idea of a mathematical genius taking the time to build a card tower fourteen stories tall. "I guess that's what kids did back then, when there were no cell phones or video games."

"What is this?" Emma asked as she walked over to a long machine with a clear tube in the middle holding an airplane wing.

"That's a wind tunnel," said Ryan. "The smoke comes out here, and it is forced over the wing by the fan in the back. You can actually see the effect of aerodynamics on many different objects by the way the smoke flows over them. This wing just happened to be left in the tunnel from yesterday.

"Don't worry. We will train you to take the students through all the experiments. It isn't as difficult as it sounds. You will be able to observe another teacher for several days and assist them before you would ever handle the class by yourself, Mrs. Harris. And with Emma to help you, I'm sure you both will be pros in no time," he added with a smile.

As they walked back out into the hallway, Emma asked, "What do the other letters stand for?"

"Well, *T* is for 'technology,' *E* is for 'engineering,' *A* is for 'art,' and *M* is for 'mathematics.' Each laboratory has activities to help students learn science and math standards," Ryan explained.

"How would they learn science in art?" Emma asked curiously.

"Would you like to see?" asked Ryan.

"Yes!" replied Emma enthusiastically.

Her mother smiled and said, "I knew you would find something here you liked!" The group followed Ryan down to the room with the large *A* above the door. Ryan turned on the light to display a large art room and an attached computer art room separated by a glass partition.

"Dr. Harris introduces students to color theory and shows them where visible light is found on the electromagnetic spectrum. Here, let me show you," he added as he walked over to a poster of the spectrum on the wall.

"The shortest waves at the start of the spectrum are gamma waves. From there, you go toward visible light to the end of the spectrum, which holds microwaves and radio waves," explained Ryan.

"You mean, color has wavelengths just like the radio waves that Dad's RC plane receives from our controller?" asked Emma.

"Yes, most fifth-grade students are amazed when they realize that visible light can be separated through a spectrum into its rainbow of colors. Each individual color has its own wavelength. Are you beginning to understand how all of these technologies interconnect?" Ryan smiled. Emma made a quizzical look, as if she still didn't quite get it.

Ryan continued, intent on having her understand how it all worked together. "Visible light operates not only with a wavelength, but also within a frequency on the electromagnetic spectrum number line." Ryan pointed again to the visual light section on the wavelength number line. "Visual light is in the center of the number line and is broken out here to display all the colors that make up visual light." He pointed to the corresponding wavelengths for each color, which were the colors a person sees in a rainbow.

"For example," he continued, "there is a reason why you see the color red in a sunset at night and blue in the sky during the day. There are many particles of dust, nitrogen, and oxygen in Earth's atmosphere that can scatter light. They can scatter blue light about ten times more than other colors, because the wavelength of the color blue is so much smaller than red's wavelength. On a clear day, when the sun is high in the sky, the color blue is the easiest to scatter. In fact, sometimes it is scattered more than once, and blue light is coming not directly from the sun but from all over the sky.

"In the evening, there is less blue light because the sun is not directly overhead emitting light, and the sky appears redder. During sunsets and sunrises, the light has to travel much farther through our atmosphere. The red wavelengths are the longest in the visual light spectrum and can travel the farthest without being scattered. Hence, we have had red sunrises and sunsets and the beautiful blue skies painted by artists for centuries." Ryan comically bowed as if he had just finished lines from one of Shakespeare's plays. Emma smiled at his theatrical ending. She could see how he would be a great teacher to explain natural phenomena that kids her age don't even think about.

"I didn't know that color was so technical," she smiled. "Do you eventually get to draw, or is it just all science?"

"Oh, yes, you learn to mix colors, or rather the paints that absorb all the colors except the one they are reflecting," he mused, "and perspective drawing, figure drawing, and still-life drawing. We just take it a step further and introduce the advanced students to 3-D computer animation and careers using that technology. As with anything else, you have to learn to walk before you can run. After our students learn the basics, they attend a demonstration and lecture by the best computer simulation experts at Wright-Patterson Air Force Base. Then, they are introduced to the need for simulators to help pilots learn to fly planes and other applications. Dr. Harris has been experimenting with virtual reality glasses and finding ways to introduce students interested in art to the basics of this new technology. Many of our students have gone to college and majored in computer-generated images applications—you've probably heard of it as 'CGI.' They help simulate pilot training and jet engine repair, and even help medical students learn surgery procedures."

"Wow, that is so cool! I think I might have found something in science that I'm interested in learning more about," Emma said as she looked up at her mom.

Sarah reached over and gave her a quick rub on her back and, with a large smile, said, "See, you are already advanced in a scientific field, and you just didn't realize it. This is just the beginning, Emma. Just think what we are going to learn this summer!"

Ryan nodded and added, "Virtual reality is really the wave of the future in many educational settings. Dr. Harris was the lead engineer at the base," he smiled, "in making the technology practical in training pilots."

Emma felt giddy inside. Maybe she wasn't as bad at science and math as she thought she was. With just these few explanations by Ryan, she already knew more today than she did this morning. Maybe she was like him in that she needed to do hands-on activities to learn and memorize something. She wondered if Grandpa would explain some of his inventions to her and help her understand science better, as Ryan did.

"Is this a 3-D printer?" Mom asked as she walked across the art room and back into the hallway.

"Yes, all of our students get a chance to either use a 3-D scanner for a small object they would like to create, or they can pick from a list we already have on the computer. We created all the counterweight trays for our broken trebuchets from a 3-D scan of another part."

Just then, the tour was interrupted by the door at the end of the hallway swinging open. It was Grandpa! He quickly walked toward them with a wide grin and shouted, "Well, hello! I knew I heard voices down here!" Suddenly, a small, brown, fluffy dog ran from behind him and barked playfully as it wagged its tail.

"A puppy!" Max exclaimed. Max ran toward Grandpa and the dog as the dog shot ahead and jumped up on him. He bent down, and it quickly licked his face, tail wagging. Emma quickly followed Max, bending down and petting the dog while he danced wildly around, barking and wagging his tail.

"Did you get a dog, Dad?" asked Mom as she gave him a hug.

"Oh, he just adopted me. I get a little lonely in the evenings when I work in my lab. He keeps me company," he smiled. "Come on over here and give your old Pappy a hug," he said as he leaned down and kissed Emma on the cheek and gave her a big bear hug. "You too, Maxwell!" He leaned down, scooped up Max, swirled him around, and kissed him on the cheek. "Do you like my new dog?"

"Where did you get him?" Max asked as he stared into Grandpa's clear blue eyes.

"I adopted him from the animal shelter. He just sat and looked at me with his big, brown eyes when I looked at all the dogs in their cages. I just knew right away that we were going to be friends. I named him Newton after Sir Isaac Newton, the famous scientist who discovered gravity. Max smiled as Grandpa put him down. Grandpa asked, "Have you all had lunch?"

"Oh, yes, Dad, we ate on our way here. We have been on a tour with Ryan. He just showed us your beautiful building. You have really done a wonderful job! I know Dave would have loved to have been here and seen it with us," she added sadly. For a moment, no one spoke as Mom looked down toward the floor and seemed to tear up.

Grandpa noticed her change in mood and quickly spoke up, "Let me show you my office. I have my own outside entrance. That way, I can come and go and not interrupt classes or activities in the hallway." The four began walking toward the end of the hall as Ryan excused himself and exited through the office door. As they entered Grandpa's office, Newton began jumping around as if he were happy to show off his new home. It was decorated with burgundy leather chairs and forest green lamps on his desk and side tables. Above his desk was a painting that Emma had not seen before. She walked over to it and stared up at the vivid colors and brush strokes. It looked like a vortex of beautiful hues and textures. Grandpa walked over, put his arm around her, and said, "Your grandma painted that for me before she died. It is my favorite of all the paintings she ever created for me," he said softly.

"What is it called? Did she give it a title?" Emma asked.

"Yes, she called it *The Unified Field*."

"What does that mean?" she asked.

"Well, for many years, I worked on trying to solve one of Einstein's most famous theories called the unified field. It is a very difficult concept that describes an invisible force that holds together and connects the electromagnetic spectrum and gravity. Einstein died without being able to solve it mathematically, and it has left many a scientist stumped who have tried to complete it for him over the years.

"One day, your grandma was reading her Bible when she looked up at me and said that the theory had already been solved. When I asked her what she meant, she read Colossians 1:17, which says, 'He is before all things, and in him all things hold together.' She said she had found the answer for me, and I could stop all my frustration and complaining," he smiled. "On my birthday the year she died, she gave this to me as a gift and told me that she never wanted me to forget the answer, no matter how much time I spent trying to prove Einstein's theory mathematically. It has been my favorite painting all these years."

"It's beautiful, Pappy," she replied but then became embarrassed that she had called him the name she gave him when she was little.

"Come on now. I know there's something left I can show you that Ryan didn't get to," Grandpa smiled as he led them back into the hallway. Newton playfully ran ahead, with Max close behind him. Emma gently shut the office door after them. She gave one last glance at her grandma's painting. It was so great to see Grandpa again and see how happy he was to show off his school. She just wished Dad could have been here with them.

3

Boiling Oil and Trebuchets

Early Monday morning of their first week of camp, Emma and her mother opened the third-floor STEAM Academy doors. The marquee lights were on, and there was a sound of laughter and talking coming from the room at the end of the hall, next to Grandpa's office. They had just dropped Max off at his classroom, and now it was their turn to step into their new adventure. Emma felt a little nervous but excited too. Babysitting was the only other job she'd had. It was kind of fun to do this with her mom, and she hoped that she might meet a new friend to spend time with this summer. It still felt a little strange to think she was actually getting paid to help other students her own age.

As they entered the office door, they were greeted by

Ryan, Grandpa, and a young woman, all in matching navy STEAM polos.

"Good morning—you made it," Grandpa said with a smile.

Ryan gave a slight wave and smile. Then he pointed to a box of donuts on the lunch table and said, "Please help yourselves if you are hungry. We will have our morning meeting in about ten minutes. The students won't arrive until a quarter to nine." Emma thanked him, picked up a glazed donut, and poured some milk as her mom poured herself a cup of coffee.

"Nicole, I'd like to introduce you to my daughter-in-law, Sarah, and my granddaughter, Emma," smiled Grandpa. Nicole, a young science education major on summer break, shook Emma's hand and then her mother's hand. She was pretty and slender, with bright red hair pulled back in a ponytail. She wore jeans with her navy STEAM polo.

"I'm so glad you are here," Nicole said. "I have been looking forward to meeting you both. I will be your teaching mentor and will train you in the Science Lab this morning. We're going to have a lot of fun, and hopefully, you will enjoy seeing the students grasp the science standards we teach them," she added. "It really is like a light going off for many of them," she smiled.

The group sat down at the long conference table, and Ryan passed out the daily schedule of classes, teachers, lunch breaks, and departure times. Emma was relieved to see that she and her mom were just going to observe and assist Nicole in the Science Lab all day. Nicole explained to them that there were four groups of students a day rotating through the STEAM classes. Dr. Harris would be helping out until Sarah could take over the Science Lab herself. Engineering and math classes were combined, and students would transition from one subject to the other halfway through their period. Dr. Harris would be teaching the engineering and math lesson at the end of the day, and this class usually had a guest speaker to talk about a relevant career goal featured in one of the classes. Today, the guest speaker would be a mechanical engineer who would discuss how robotics aids the assembly line process.

Grandpa read the name of the guest speaker and said, "A local robotics company has loaned us a robotic arm. The speaker today is from that company and will explain a little about programming, majors and programs associated with his career, the benefits of robotics to businesses, and the impact on global competition. This is one of my favorite businesses in the area, because the company works so closely with community colleges and career centers. It has even reached out to some of our most at risk students and have given them summer jobs to help them get a vision for their futures. In fact, the company has hired some of our former students."

Grandpa glanced over at Emma and Sarah, pleased to share with them some of the school's former success stories. Emma was so proud of her grandpa. In some ways, she felt like a celebrity because of the way people treated her whenever they found out she was his granddaughter. She felt so special to be asked to help with the school for the summer. She just hoped she wouldn't let him down in any way.

Grandpa looked at Ryan and asked, "Have all the slots for guest speakers been filled for the entire week?"

Ryan nodded and replied, "Yes, they have, but I had to make a change in the speaker for today due to a scheduling conflict. Colonel Wayman will be filling in with a lecture about cybersecurity. The robotics lecture has been moved back to Friday. Everyone else has confirmed their time, and I will start next week's lineup."

"Wonderful," replied Grandpa. "Thank you for taking care of that. Sounds like we are off to a great start." He looked at Emma and her mom as he continued, "The second-floor crew will take over during lunch, so once the students are dropped off, you can come back upstairs and eat. Everyone grab your radio, clip it on, and don't hesitate to call me or Ryan if you need any help," he added.

As they all rose from the conference table, Grandpa reached over, gave Emma a sideways hug, and looked down at her, saying, "I have some time set aside for you before lunch. I want to show you one of my new inventions using virtual reality glasses. It is a program I wrote called Women of STEM. I think you will really like it. I made it just for you. I thought I could show you how it works; it is just a prototype and is connected to my office computer. We can also talk about anything you have questions about concerning science. How does that sound to you?"

Emma nodded her head and replied rather downcast, "Sounds great, except I didn't do very well in school this year."

"I know," replied Grandpa, "but that is behind you. You can pick up some STEAM this summer and be at the head of your class in no time."

"Do you really think so?" asked Emma.

"I know so. You're a Harris. Aren't you?" he winked.

Just then, a female voice from the second floor came over the radio, telling Ryan that the buses had arrived and the students would be on the steps in five minutes. Ryan replied, "Okay, we're ready," as he reached over to a knob under a speaker and turned on patriotic music, which filled the hallways. "We always like to set the mood and help them feel special as they enter their homerooms and start their day," said Ryan. Nicole motioned for Emma and her mother to stand with her at the entrance of the Science Lab, under the S sign, just as the door swung open with another navy polo–clad worker from the second floor. The worker smiled and explained to his group which rooms would be their homerooms and where to place their lunch bags.

The excited students obediently placed their lunches on the carts by their homeroom doors and went inside. In the Science Lab, Nicole instructed the students to line up along the wall for attendance, which she took while pointing out each student's seat and informing them of their teams for the day. As the tables filled up, Nicole motioned for Emma to take a seat with a team missing a fourth person.

"This will be a good way for you to learn the procedures and the experiments. You can just be part of a team. Is that okay with you?" she smiled.

"Yes," answered Emma.

Nicole motioned to Emma's mother to sit near the front of the room and said, "Sarah, why don't you sit in this chair next to my smartboard, so you can see the PowerPoint presentation." Emma had been seated next to a girl with long, black braids. The two boys across from them briefly glanced at her and the girl seated next to her before Nicole began her introduction. The photo on Nicole's PowerPoint introduction slide showed students with goggles working on a bottle rocket. The word "STEAM" was written across the top of the slide.

"Hello, and welcome to the STEAM Academy! My name is Ms. Nicole. I would like to welcome you to your first day of camp. You are going to make a lot of friends and learn a lot about science, technology, engineering, art, and math. That's what our acronym 'STEAM' represents."

The next slide showed photos of Emma's grandpa in his US Air Force uniform and as a civilian in front of the Pentagon. Nicole introduced him to the students as Dr. Harris and described his service as an engineer in the US Air Force, his interest in education, and his dream to create a program to reinforce fifth-grade science standards and give kids a vision for their futures. She showed a photo of him in his laboratory and another with him seated at a large table with representatives from the military and Congress. She went on to say how he thought it was important for our country's young people to grasp science standards at a young age and for communities to get involved to mentor and model careers of the future.

Emma was amazed at how many people Grandpa's program included. Teachers, scientists, and businesses all volunteered and received either continuing educational units or corresponding business perks and tax credits for giving their time and resources to help students succeed in their communities.

The next slide showed the rules for the program. Many were like school rules:

1. Students had to raise their hands before asking questions.
2. Students were not supposed to talk while the teacher was talking.
3. Until they were instructed to, students were not to touch any of the supplies on the tables when entering a new lab.

Nicole had the students look up at the ceiling to see their table's name. Every table was named after a famous inventor or scientist. Emma smiled, as her group was called the Einstein group. She remembered the trouble Einstein had in school when he was young and thought to herself how appropriate this group was for her. Nicole explained that this inventor was their team's name and that they would be able to easily find their seats in any lab by looking for his photo and name hanging from the ceiling in the lab.

Nicole also had the students look at the numbers written on their chairs. Each chair in their group had a number of one through four. Nicole explained that these numbers were important. Each instructor used them. When an instructor called out a number from each team, the instructor would be asking the person sitting in the chair with that number to get up or go get supplies in an experiment.

Nicole asked each student to take a STEAM notebook from the center of the table and write their name on it and their table's name. She explained that each student's notebook was their own, but they were not allowed to take them home until the end of the week. The notebook contained all of the experiments they would do to help them understand their fifth-grade physical science standards. The notebook would be a souvenir of their week, with information on the careers they had learned about.

The students were then told to write their names on the color-coded name tags in front of them, which were attached to lanyards, and to put them on. The name tags had a number in the upper right-hand corner. Nicole explained that this was the number of the bus they would ride back to the YMCA and that their parents would pick them up right away or after extended care.

Emma was amazed at how organized all of these details were and thought that Ryan must have come up with all these groups, colors, and ways to keep everyone organized. He was so cool and really cute too. She wondered if he or Ms. Nicole were dating anyone. Emma smiled at the thought of them someday being a married couple who taught together. They would make a "dynamic duo," as her dad used to call Grandma and Grandpa.

After everyone put on their name tags, they were given five minutes to introduce themselves to the person next to them. Nicole told them they had to introduce themselves and share their favorite hobby or interest and what they wanted to be when they graduated, if they knew that already.

The girl seated next to Emma quickly turned to her and

said, "Hi, my name is Shania." She gave Emma a warm smile and continued, "I live in Trotwood, about twenty-five minutes from here. I really like science. My mother works on the base in a research lab and thought I would learn a lot from this camp. I would really like to be an astronaut someday. What about you?"

Emma smiled back and said, "My name is Emma, and we moved here from Arizona two months ago. Dr. Harris is my grandfather. We live about ten minutes from here, in Beavercreek. I don't know what I want to do when I'm older, and I really like to ride horses."

"Wow, Dr. Harris is your grandfather?" asked Shania. "Are you as smart as he is?"

"No, not really. I think my mom and grandpa are hoping that this program will help me," replied Emma.

"I think it's going to be fun," Shania said with a smile.

Just then, Nicole caught their attention with three claps. Nicole smiled and said, "When you hear three claps, I want you to respond with three claps. Let's try it." Nicole clapped again, and that was followed by an explosive response of claps from the students. "Good," she replied. "That will be our signal to return our attention to the entire class when you have broken off into your groups to work. Okay, let's get started," said Nicole. She reached over, started a different slideshow, and asked a student to turn off the lights. The first slide showed a castle wall filled with men with bows and arrows. A catapult prepared to attack the wall with a fiery ball about to be launched.

Nicole began the lecture by pointing at the archers and stating, "Over centuries, armies continually advanced their ability to hurl fire or shoot missiles to attack their adversaries. Bows and arrows were invented to give armies an advantage in attacking their enemies from a distance. In this picture, we have a ballista, which is a form of crossbow. Many of these torsion-powered arrow firers had been used since 400 BC, and the technique had been adapted from using stones as projectiles."

Nicole forwarded the slide to the next image and said, "This next slide is a drawing of a wooden catapult. It is called a trebuchet. There are smaller-scaled versions along the window, which we will use in a little while. The trebuchet was an advanced development of the twelfth or thirteen century. Its ability to throw larger objects and create more damage to castle walls was due to the counterweight system. This ability to throw burning mixtures, diseased animals, or heavy boulders could break down any fortress or introduce disease to kill the inhabitants protected behind the walls. The range of the trebuchet kept the attackers a safe distance from archers or any boiling oil that could be poured down on them. This weapon was the major siege engine until the development of the canon."

The next slide featured a man with long, white hair. "This is Sir Isaac Newton," said Nicole. He discovered the laws of motion. We're going to talk a lot about him today. His second law of motion, associated with the destructive power of the trebuchet, is written simply as F = M x A, which stands for 'force is equal to mass times acceleration.' That may not mean anything to you right now, but in a few moments, we will do an activity that will help you understand it completely.

"Newton's laws and principles of force and motion are a major standard you are expected to learn and master in the fifth grade. I would really like you to try to memorize his name and try to remember his three laws of motion, which we will explain to you this week."

Shania glanced quickly back at Emma and giggled as she whispered, "Look at his hair!"

Emma smiled back and quickly focused again on the

lecture. Nicole pointed at the dates under his portrait as she continued, "Isaac Newton was born in England on December twenty-fifth in 1642 and died on March twentieth in 1727." The next slide displayed pictures of the many inventions and discoveries that Newton made in his lifetime. "In my opinion, Sir Isaac Newton has made more contributions to the advancement of scientific knowledge than any other scientist. This is just my opinion, but let me explain."

Nicole pointed to the photo of the solar system. "Through Newton's laws of motion and universal gravitation—which explain the trajectories of comets, the tides, and equinoxes—he helped to remove any doubts in the scientific community about the validity of the heliocentric model of the solar system. In other words, he proved once and for all that Earth and the other planets in our solar system rotated around the sun and how gravity played a major role in this motion of objects on Earth and other planets.

"He also proved that Earth was an oblate spheroid, or round with flattening at the poles. He published the *Principia* in 1687, which proved that the flattening at the poles depends on the density and the balance of gravitational force and centrifugal force. For example, giant gas planets like Jupiter and Saturn are flattened by rotation more than Earth is.

"Those are just a few of many discoveries!" Nicole said with an amazed tone. "He also built the first practical reflecting telescope, and he discovered that white light could be separated through a prism into the colors of the visible spectrum. Along with his contributions to mathematical sciences, Newton made the first theoretical calculation of the speed of sound. He was knighted by Queen Anne in 1705 and spent the last three decades of his life in London, serving as warden of the Royal Mint and president of the Royal Society."

Nicole paused for dramatic effect as she looked around the room. Slowly, she said, "Can you imagine someone, in one lifetime, being able to discover and explain all of these invisible forces that had been acting on our world for centuries? Forces hidden from ordinary people who went through their lives benefiting from gravity and the equinoxes of our planet but never realizing that there were constant, physical laws that could be harnessed and calculated for trajectories of rockets to launch satellites someday?"

She smiled and held up her smartphone. "Scientists were able to use Newton's equations to launch rockets to place satellites around the earth. Because of Newton's laws of motion, I can send a signal to a satellite orbiting the earth that will enable me to bounce a signal off of it to Mrs. Sarah here." She then pressed a button, and after a few seconds, Emma's mom's phone rang. She replied, "Hello, Ms. Nicole."

Looking at the class, Nicole ended her slideshow with, "You see, boys and girls, it is so important that you understand the invisible laws of physics around you. Someday, you may build on the discoveries of others and develop vaccines, new sources of energy, and nanoengineering I can't even imagine—but *you* will!"

She motioned for the same student to turn on the lights, and she looked around the room. "Let's start with your fifth-grade milestone of forces and motion. Both can be explained by Sir Isaac Newton's three laws of motion, which he developed in 1686, exactly twenty years after he developed his theories on gravity."

Nicole reached over to her computer once more to bring up a document listing all three laws. "Now," she began, "I want you to read the first law with me."

The class began to read aloud together, "An object will remain at rest or in uniform motion in a straight line unless compelled to change its state by the action of an external force."

"What does that mean?" asked Nicole. "Well, I'd like person number one from each table to take the two plastic cars out from the caddy in the center of your table. Place one car between each set of partners at your table." Shania reached into the caddy and handed one car to the two boys across their table and placed the other between her and Emma.

"Now," continued Nicole, "is that car moving? Anyone can answer."

"No," came the class's reply.

"That's right," said Nicole, "and it won't move unless you push it with your finger along the table. This is an example of an object at rest that will stay at rest until force is applied to it.

"In my hand, I have a marble. If I were to roll this marble down the hallway outside, at the double-door entrance you used this morning, all the way to Dr. Harris's office, do you think it would eventually stop or keep moving?" Shania raised her hand. Nicole smiled at her and said, "Yes, what do you think?"

"I think it would stop because of gravity," said Shania.

"Yes, that is right, but there would be one more force acting upon it to slow it down and eventually cause it to stop. Does anyone know what that force would be?"

Emma wished she could raise her hand and answer, but she really didn't know what it could be. She had seen her dad's airplane brought to a complete stop in the air if not given more power when it flew into the wind, but she wasn't sure if what happened in a hallway was the same.

"Let me put it this way," continued Nicole. "There is a fluid filling up our hallway that has roughly fifteen pounds per square inch at sea level. The metric equivalent would be 453 grams per square inch. It is invisible, and you have lived in it your entire lives, as you walk through it every day." She smiled. "Does anyone know what I am talking about?" Emma raised her hand. "Yes, Emma?" asked Nicole.

"Is it air?" asked Emma timidly.

"Yes! Good job!" smiled Nicole. "Air is a fluid like water. It fills the container that it is in. Air causes friction on anything moving through it. Together with gravity, the air in the hallway would act as a force on the object in motion—which, in our case, would be our marble—and would eventually bring it to a complete stop.

"Now, if we were in space, a space probe that was set in motion would keep moving through space because it has no friction to slow it down. There is no air and no gravitational pull if you're not near a planet or moon. Even if a space probe did not have any fuel, it could travel a long distance by inertia. Does anyone know what 'inertia' is?" Nicole asked. The class was silent, and no one raised their hand.

"The tendency of an object to resist any change in motion is called 'inertia,'" explained Nicole. "Objects that have a lot of mass and that are heavier have more inertia than objects of less mass. Still objects in inertia do not want to move, and moving objects in inertia resist changes while moving in a straight line.

"Let me give you an example," she smiled. "When you are riding in a car and the car makes a sharp turn, the inertia of your body will resist the change, and you will lean against the car door as if you were still moving in a straight line. Or if you were riding along in that car and you went over a hill at a high speed, your body would want to continue moving along that path, and you feel the sensation of going up when the car moves over the hill. Has anyone felt that before? Just raise your hand if you have." Everyone raised their hand. "Well, that is an example of Newton's first law of motion," said Nicole.

"Okay, let's move on to his second law of motion." Nicole pointed up at the screen. "This is where we get to have some fun with the trebuchets!" she smiled. "In Newton's second law, he explains how force is the product of mass and acceleration. The force acting on an object can cause the object to speed up, slow down, or change direction. The formula is written as *F* equals *M* times *A*.

"Now, Newton's second law also states that the greater the force applied, the greater the change in motion for a given mass. In other words, a large force will produce more acceleration than a small force acting on the same object."

Nicole showed a split-screen picture of two boats moving across a lake and a photo of a large motor on the opposite side. One boat was a lightweight rowboat, and the other was a heavier cruise ship. "Now, raise your hand, and using Newton's second law of motion, tell me which mass, or boat, will accelerate at a greater speed when the force of this motor is applied to the back of it?" Nicole asked.

A boy raised his hand. Nicole pointed to him and said, "Go ahead."

He lowered his hand and answered, "I think the rowboat would just take off if you put that motor on the back of it, versus the heavier boat with people on it."

"You are absolutely right," smiled Nicole. "Each boat would be powered with the same force, but the weight of the rowboat would allow it to move more quickly than the heavier passenger boat. But the same principle can apply to heavy objects slowing down, as in the case of a heavy truck on the highway. Larger masses are harder to accelerate and harder to stop. Even truck drivers have to be aware of Newton's second law of motion to drive safely," said Nicole.

"Okay, I would now like person number two at each table to raise your hands." Emma raised her hand, along with the number two person from the other tables. "When I signal you, I want you to go over to the windowsill, bring back a trebuchet, and place it in the middle of your table. Please carry it from the bottom with two hands, so you don't release the pin holding the sling in place. Team members, please do not touch it until I explain all the moving parts and assign roles for our experimentation. Okay, number twos, go and get your table's trebuchet," said Nicole.

Emma went over to the windowsill and picked up the closest trebuchet to her table. She carefully brought it back and placed it in the center of the table. Everyone began talking about it and pointing to different parts.

Clap-clap-clap came the sound from Nicole. The class responded with claps and became quiet. "Good job following instructions," she said. "Now look at my example as I point out all the moving parts. Open your STEAM notebook to page eleven. Look at the illustration of a trebuchet and the corresponding parts as I identify them and how they are used in Newton's second law. First of all, the entire trebuchet is described as a lever. Levers are used to lift objects or fling them, as our trebuchet here does. It has four parts: the lever arm, the load, the effort, and the fulcrum.

"The lever arm pivots on an axle. On the short end of the lever arm is a massive counterweight. Attached to the long end of the arm is a rope sling, which can hold a projectile, such as a big stone. Because the counterweight outweighs the stone, sometimes being as much as fifty times heavier, the short end hangs down and the sling end is elevated while the trebuchets are at rest.

"It was no easy task to add a counterweight to a trebuchet in the field. In medieval times, there must have been dozens of soldiers pulling on ropes to load it. Once loaded with a heavy counterweight, the lever now has the effort of the load. That's what makes the counterweight swing. The pivot point of the arm is the fulcrum. In our case, because the trebuchet's fulcrum is located between the load and the effort, a trebuchet is considered a first-class lever.

"Look at the firing pin," Nicole continued. "This would have ropes attached to it so that soldiers could pull on the ropes to remove it. When it is removed, the sling end accelerates, and the centrifugal force is generated, causing the sling and its stone to swing outward in an arc of its own.

"When the trebuchet reaches its full height, it will stop, while the sling will continue to accelerate as it swings upward. When the sling is nearly vertical, it will release the stone and send it on a trajectory toward the target, which might be a city wall or an enemy army.

"You can imagine," said Nicole, "that there had to be many adjustments to the mass of the stone or counterweight to be able to hit a target. The people who made these adjustments were considered specialists in their roles in the launch, assuring accuracy and building on what they learned.

"This brings me to your assignments. I would like person number one at each table to take out the plastic bag filled with clay balls from the caddy in the center of your table and place it in front of you. You are the projectile loader. Your job is to make sure that you place the correct clay balls of different masses in the trebuchet at the proper times of your launches.

"Everyone look at the chart you will be filling in. On the first launch, you will use the red clay ball, which has a mass of fifteen grams. On the second launch, you will use the green clay ball, which is twenty grams, and on your third launch, you will use the yellow clay ball, which is twenty-five grams. Don't open the bag until everyone has their assignments and you are assigned a space either here in the room or in the hallway.

"Okay, person number two, you are the arming specialist

and will lower the long arm of the trebuchet and put in the trigger pin to secure it before the counterweight is put in. Person number three, you are the counterweight specialist and will add in the counterweight, labeled two hundred grams, for your first set of launches. After going through all the clay balls and measuring your distances, you will add an additional fifty grams of weight and do your entire experiment again.

“Everyone look up at me,” Nicole smiled. “Mrs. Harris and I will place a small plastic castle exactly five meters away from your trebuchet after you place it on the floor. Your goal is to experiment with your different projectile masses and counterweight masses and record which clay ball lands closest to or hits your target, which is the toy castle. Person number four, you are the measurement specialist. Your job is to measure from the base of your trebuchet to the point where the clay ball hits the floor and give that measurement to your teammates to record on the chart in their STEAM notebooks.

“You will have twenty-five minutes to work through all your projectile clay weights with your two sets of counterweights to find the best combination to hit your target. The team that finishes, has clear and concise information, and stays on task in their assigned roles will receive points, which will be applied to your overall weekly scores. These points can earn you a STEAM pennant and award at the end of the week. Are there any questions?” asked Nicole.

“Okay, I will take the teams on this side of the room into the hallway and assign your launch spots, and Mrs. Harris will stay in here with the row next to the windows and have you spread out along the three aisles. Everyone, at this time, put on your safety glasses. Number ones, carry the clay projectile plastic bag. Number twos, pick up the trebuchets. Number threes, carry the counterweights, and number fours, carry everyone's folders, pencils, and your tape measures. Let's get started!"

Within minutes, Emma's group was on the floor in the aisle next to the windows, and everyone seemed excited to get the trebuchet working. Emma's mother measured five meters away from their launch site and placed the brown plastic castle. Shania and Emma laughed, as there were even tiny soldiers with tiny bows and arrows on top of the castle wall facing them.

Emma pulled down on the counterweight tray and placed the trigger pin as Shania put the first clay ball in the sling. One of the boys in her group, named Steven, placed the first counterweight in the tray, and his friend Josh began counting down, "Three, two, one!"

Emma pulled out the firing pin. The clay ball was launched, made an arch into the air, but fell a few feet in front of the castle. Steven measured their distance, and the team quickly recorded the mass of the projectile and counterweight and distance in their Launch #1 chart.

With each launch and change of mass, they saw that the distance decreased if the projectile became heavier. They had fun working together as a team and soon started the second phase of the experiment, adding another fifty grams to the counterweight tray. This began with the first clay ball.

"Three, two, one!" shouted Josh as he pulled the pin. The first launch, with the lightest mass, flew over the top of the castle and landed a few feet behind it. They all recorded the distance that was called out to the team, and then they tried the second clay mass. This time, the combination of the green clay ball weighing twenty grams and the counterweight mass of 250 grams created a projectile arch that made a direct hit on the castle! Emma looked at Shania and raised her hands in victory as their team let out a yell. They did it!

"Keep working," said Mrs. Harris, "You have only three minutes left to reposition the castle and fire the last clay projectile with the 250 grams of counterweight effort. If you run out of time, you won't earn your points!"

Emma's team quickly repositioned the castle, and everyone performed their roles to launch and record the last clay ball, which landed in front of the castle. They had just finished their charts when the timer went off, and Nicole poked her head in from the hallway. She then told everyone to stop any more launches.

Emma and Shania laughed and fist-bumped Josh and Steven as they brought their trebuchet back to their table and put all the clay balls and counterweights away in the caddy on their table.

Nicole quickly made her way to the front of the room and brought up the PowerPoint slide of Newton's second law: force equals mass times acceleration. "Okay," she began, "I would like someone to explain to me how this principle worked in the trebuchet experiment and how you finally were able to hit your target." Steven raised his hand. "Yes, go ahead," said Nicole.

"Well, we first tried all the different clay weights with the counterweight that weighed two hundred grams and found that the mass did not accelerate with enough force to reach the castle walls. We then added fifty grams of counterweight to make two hundred fifty grams in the tray and had enough force used with the second clay ball that weighed twenty grams to hit the castle wall and send it flying under the table," explained Steven.

"Good," replied Nicole. "Hopefully, you all observed that by adjusting the different masses, you would have different outcomes in reaching your target. Now let's go back to medieval wartime. If you wanted a really heavy boulder to do the most damage to your enemy's castle wall, you would have to have a really heavy counterweight.

"Can you imagine how many soldiers with ropes it must have taken to load the counterweight tray with a mass sometimes fifty times heavier than the boulder and to keep it lowered until the trigger pin could be inserted? I'm sure it must have taken many tries and required moving the trebuchet to find the right distance out of the archers' reach yet be close enough to hit the castle wall with a force that could do damage.

"At this time, I want you all to put your safety glasses and pencils back in the center of the table. When I call your table, line up at the door to get ready to go to your next class in the computer lab. You won't be sitting as a team there, but we will have you regroup for further experiments later on in the day." Nicole motioned for Mrs. Harris to lead the students out of the room and across the hall. She stopped Emma and told her that she was to go to Dr. Harris's office now to meet her grandpa.

Emma obediently picked up her folder and whispered to Shania that she would catch up with her a little later. Shania responded, "Okay, I'll be looking for you." Emma stayed with her line until the entrance to the computer lab and continued walking to the open door of her grandpa's office. She saw a small brown fluff of fur run across the entrance, and her heart leaped with the realization that Newton was here too.

4

Deep Magic

Though the Witch knew the Deep Magic, there is a magic deeper still which she did not know. Her knowledge goes back only to the dawn of Time.

C. S. Lewis, *The Lion, the Witch, and the Wardrobe*

As Emma walked through Grandpa's door, Newton ran over and jumped on her to be petted. His paws barely reached her knees, so she bent down on one knee and hugged him, saying, "Hi Newton! I'm so glad you came today!" She looked up at Grandpa and asked, "Do you bring him every day?"

Grandpa smiled and replied, "Not every day, but when I know I will be working late, he keeps me company. He climbs the stairs really well, and we take breaks together and walk along the river. He's a really good walking buddy," he smiled.

Grandpa was sitting at his desk. The computer was on, and he had pulled up a chair next to him. He had a pair of virtual reality (VR) glasses on his desk.

"Come over here and sit down, Emma. I have something I want to show you."

Emma sat down and looked at the black headset.

Grandpa typed in the name of his program on his laptop computer and waited for it to open while he turned to look at Emma. "When your mom and dad told me about how you had lost interest in school and were struggling to keep your grades up, I began creating this program so that you could meet women who made great contributions as scientists and mathematicians.

"I have programmed my computer to be interactive with you and answer any of your questions. You will also see current jobs that female scientists do at the Air Force Research Lab. I thought that might help you to see a vision of yourself in a scientific field if you get interested in science. How does that sound?"

"It sounds really great!" smiled Emma. "How does it work?"

"Well," said Grandpa, "to begin with, I want you to carry the glasses and follow me into the lab. I will show you where the glasses work."

Emma quickly picked up the glasses and followed Grandpa through another set of doors to a room he called his Virtual Reality Lab. Newton trotted ahead, stopping at the outside door, where he lay down on a rug. The room held a large, white cube that looked as if it were about ten feet wide and ten feet high. It was open at the front, with a pair of funny slippers on the floor, positioned at the entrance.

"You will have to put on these slippers, so the soles of

your tennis shoes won't hurt the material on the floor," said Grandpa.

Emma hurriedly sat down in a nearby chair, slipped on the big slippers, and stood next to Grandpa at the entrance of the white cube.

"I know you have heard of the green screens that are used in movie productions. An actor can move or hang from the ceiling in front of a green screen, and producers can add video or any computer-generated image that they would like to have in the background. This white screen is similar in that it allows more complex, interactive 3-D images to move and be manipulated while you wear the VR glasses. This is where you will stand to see the program I created for you to meet Grace."

"Grace?" asked Emma curiously.

"Grace is the name of my computer. I have patterned her after Grace Hopper. Hopper was a famous computer engineer and mathematician. In the program, my computer can actually talk to you in the virtual image of Grace Hopper. She was one of the first scientists to create the computer and computer language. Have you ever heard the term 'computer bug'? Well, Grace Hopper was the computer scientist who coined that term. She will explain to you all of her accomplishments," smiled Grandpa.

Grandpa held the headset and pointed to a button on the right side. "Now, this is important. You can stop and start the program at any time by pressing this button. Grace will save your spot, and you can pick up where you left off if you would like to continue the program later. You have my permission to come in here and continue the program in between classes or after lunch. All I ask is that you take great care in making sure all the doors are locked on your way out and that you make sure Newton won't get out if he is left in here during sessions."

Emma looked up and said, "Yes, I will be very careful."

"Good. I knew I could count on you. Let's get started. Are you ready to begin?"

Emma nodded with enthusiasm and said, "Yes!"

Grandpa pointed to a line on the floor where she should stand within the cube for the best effect of the program. "Always wear your shoe protectors to protect the material and step up to that spot on the floor. Then, just put on the headset and turn it on. When you are finished, just step back to the chair, take off the protectors, and slip them under the chair for safekeeping. You can rest the headset on this table and cover it with this plastic to keep the dust out of the components."

Emma gingerly stepped onto the floor of the VR simulator. Before putting on the headgear, she looked back at her grandfather in awe and said curiously, "Grandpa, how did you do all of this? How have you stayed so interested in science all of these years and created this school and these programs to help kids like me learn science this way?"

"Okay, step back off the cube floor and let's sit for a moment. I can't answer that in a few seconds," he chuckled. Grandpa took a step back and sat in a chair next to the one Emma had used to put on her slippers. She sat next to him and eagerly anticipated his answer.

"Emma, the only way I can explain to you my interest in physics and math is by way of an analogy. Do you remember reading the series of books by C. S. Lewis titled *The Chronicles of Narnia*?"

"Yes, I loved those books. The lion statue outside of the school reminded me of Aslan in the story," smiled Emma.

"Well, in his books, C. S. Lewis refers to the 'Deep Magic' that was created at the creation of the world. Rules and laws that were part of the fabric of how our world spins and of the constant and unchanging nature of gravity and the electromagnetic spectrum. For me, as a small boy, I wanted to learn as much about these laws, put into place by our Creator, as I could. It was like I was discovering ancient wisdom that could not be changed or moved.

"Throughout the centuries, these laws of physics have helped us to discover energy, medicine, and ways to care for all the people on our planet. Just like in the story, as Lucy learned more about the Deep Magic of Narnia, she learned more about the deep love of Aslan for the inhabitants of Narnia."

He looked sincerely at Emma and continued, "Science has allowed me to take a look at the majesty of our Creator. The more I learn and discover, the more I realize we have only glimpsed the tip of the iceberg of scientific discoveries."

Grandpa put his hand on her shoulder as he continued, "Teaching is my gift. I experience my greatest joy when I impart this love of knowledge to students who might never understand the beauty of these gifts of creation. In a way, I feel that education is my highest calling and the reason why I invent.

"Does that make sense to you?" he asked as he looked down at the VR glasses.

"Yes, it does," she replied. "I'm so proud of you, Grandpa, and I want to be just like you!"

He hugged her and kissed her on the cheek. "Then let's get started, young lady. Grace has a lot to show you! I have to go over to the base today, so when you are finished, turn off the lights and make sure to shut my office door behind you. You can come in any time you have free time to talk to Grace and continue her program about Women of STEM. It might take you several days to finish the program. I want you to stop if it gets overwhelming with too much information. You have to give yourself time to process the information, and I really want you to have fun doing it!" he smiled as he stood up.

"Okay, I will, and thank you, Grandpa!" she smiled. He patted her on the back and walked out of the room with Newton at his heels. Emma put the slippers back on and stepped into the white VR cube. She put on the headset and pressed the On button.

5

Virtual Reality and Women of STEM

Emma heard the click of Grandpa's office door shut as the blackness of the VR glasses became a blurred room that slowly came into focus. Her senses were flooded with loud clicking sounds as a wall of cabinets eight feet high appeared. Ten feet from her was a middle-aged woman with light brown hair pulled back into a bun. She wore dark-rimmed glasses, a white suit jacket with a matching skirt that came down to her knees, and high heels. She stood with her back to Emma and faced the wall of cabinets, which contained huge reels of tape that were spinning behind glass. There were buttons flashing. The woman slowly turned after pushing a button and closing a cabinet. With a kind smile, she said, "Welcome to my laboratory, Emma. I'm so glad to have this opportunity to meet you. My name is Dr. Grace Hopper. Please call me Grace."

She walked toward Emma and extended her hand. Emma slowly put her hand forward and saw the handshake between the two of them. Though she felt nothing, seeing it, she thought, "This VR program feels so real." She was rather embarrassed at how slowly she had responded to the handshake while Grace had stood patiently with her hand extended.

"I am your grandfather's personal computer. I am designed with artificial intelligence capabilities and can respond to you in a natural manner. I was a gift from the United States Department of Defense to Dr. Harris upon his retirement. I am to aid him in his virtual reality experiments for education. The program you are experiencing now was written to help girls in middle school see the contributions of female scientists throughout the centuries and to see current jobs in STEAM fields that are in high demand. I can take you anywhere in time or space to show you some of the women who have made great contributions to science."

Emma could not believe how real Grace seemed. She looked like a real human professor, yet the handshake reminded her that Grace was not really there.

"May I ask you a question?" Emma asked rather shyly.

"Yes," Grace replied.

"How old are you, and what is the machine behind you?"

"You have been placed in my life at a time when I was thirty-eight years old and was working at Harvard University for the navy. I had just earned my PhD at Yale and was hired at Harvard to work on the Mark I computer with Howard Aiken. What you see behind me is the Mark I. It is the first machine classified as a relay computer. I worked on it with two other scientists under the direction of Howard Aiken. It was fifty-five feet long and eight feet high. It weighed approximately five tons. It was used by the navy for gunnery and ballistic calculations and was in operation until 1959."

Emma's eyes grew wide as she said, "You mean, this was a computer?"

"Yes," replied Grace. "It may look like a dinosaur-age machine to you today, but in the late 1940s, this was cutting-edge technology. It allowed our country to have the upper hand against foreign adversaries. What the calculator function on your phone can do instantaneously in solving mathematical problems, the Mark I would do in three to five seconds," smiled Grace.

"Wow," said Emma slowly, "so this is what the first

Grace Hopper, Bureau of Ordnance's Computation Project at Harvard University, 1941 (Courtesy of the United States Navy.)

computer looked like?" Turning to look at Grace again, she said, "Can you show me what your life was like when you were my age and other things that you developed?"

"Hold my hand," responded Grace, "as I take you back to my childhood. If you begin to get dizzy, just shut your eyes."

Emma put her hand out again to hold Grace's hand, only to feel her own fingers against her palm. The room Grace stood in began to dissolve as a new image appeared. Emma found herself in a small bedroom looking at a small girl sitting on the floor. The girl held the back of a clock. Springs, screws, and small metal parts were on the rug where she sat.

"When I was a young girl," began Grace, "I was really curious about how clocks worked and kept time. One day, I took one of our family clocks to my room, took the back off, and removed all of the pieces. I found it fascinating that gears and springs could keep accurate time. The only problem with this experiment is that I couldn't get the pieces back together again when I was finished. I ended up dismantling seven clocks in our house," Grace chuckled as she looked over at Emma.

"My parents wanted to encourage my interests. My grandfather was a civil engineer in New York, and he took me with him when he surveyed bridges and other projects he was working on." Grace held her hand out again and said, "Let me show you my grandfather and how he made an impact on my life, much like Dr. Harris has done for you."

Emma reached out her hand, and the room dissolved again. The new image showed a small girl wearing a coat, hat, stockings, and black buckled shoes and standing beside an older man in an overcoat. They were looking through what Emma thought must be some kind of surveying equipment. They stood on a hillside overlooking a bridge and a river. A bustling harbor in the background was filled with barges docked at piers with storage buildings. Men on the dock used cranes to load and unload boxes and crates onto wagons.

Grace looked over at Emma and said, "I really enjoyed accompanying my grandfather on his surveying trips. It was during those trips that I developed an interest in geometry and engineering. My grandfather explained to me some of the mathematical formulas he used and how stress on bridges was relieved by the placement of steel beams under them, stretching across an expanse of water. I realized for the first time how these laws of physics could be used in many different applications. I wanted to be able to use these rules and laws and understand how to apply them as my grandfather did." Grace reached out her hand again, which was a signal to Emma that the room would dissolve again into a different time in Grace's life.

Emma saw Grace as a young woman sitting in a room with many other students. Most of them were young men. Grace continued, "My mother had studied math and encouraged me to pursue my interests in engineering and math. This was not a normal pursuit for girls in my day, but my mother was intent on giving me the same education that my brother had."

Grace looked over to Emma and said, "I too have experienced failure in school in some degree. This is the day I took my entrance exam for Vassar College. I failed the test that day because of my low scores in Latin. I didn't give up. I studied, retook the test the following year, and passed. I earned my bachelor's degree in mathematics and physics in 1928."

Emma looked at her and said, "I can't imagine you failing anything."

"Oh, yes, I did fail the entrance exam, but I didn't let that failure hold me back. I used it to take a year off and study. I knew I would pass the following year after applying myself, and I did!" smiled Grace. "I went on to earn my master's degree from Yale University in 1930 and began working on my doctoral degree at the same time that I began working for Vassar College in 1931. Three years later, I earned my PhD from Yale University."

"Wow!" exclaimed Emma. "You ended up working for the university whose entrance exam you had failed."

"Yes, that's right," smiled Grace. "Now you are beginning to understand that a person is limited by her past failures only if she allows herself to be. I failed my entrance test into college, but I didn't let that end my dreams of learning more about mathematics and physics. It just delayed me for one year while I studied harder to pass. Your past failures don't define you, Emma. You mustn't give up. You might go on to have greater accomplishments than your father or grandfather. Sometimes, it just takes a step back and determination to try again."

Grace extended her hand toward Emma for one final time jump. As Emma reached out her hand, she couldn't stop thinking about how this amazing woman had once failed at an important test.

The room dissolved and was brought back into focus again in the noisy room filled with large cabinets full of reel tape and clicking lights and buttons. Grace turned toward Emma as she began to relay the rest of her life and accomplishments. "I was working as a math professor at Vassar College when the United States entered the Second World War. In 1943, I quit my job to join the Women Accepted for Volunteer Emergency Service, also known as WAVES. Even though I was too small to meet the physical requirements, I guess they decided that my mathematical expertise was something that our country needed. I was thrilled to be accepted because my great-grandfather had also been in the navy. The navy assigned me to Harvard University, where, as I mentioned, I worked to program one of the first electronic computers."

Grace briefly chuckled, looked over at Emma, and said, "I remember thinking to myself that it was the prettiest gadget I had ever seen," smiled Grace. "My team was assigned to solve equations for the military that were too complicated to be done by a large group of people. One of these equations was the implosion equation for the Manhattan Project, which was the code name for the atomic bomb developed during the Second World War.

"After the war, I continued working with computers and decided that we needed a way to 'talk' to them using English. During this time, programmers used complicated binary code to program. Of course, everyone thought I was being naïve to try to talk to computers, but I proved them wrong. You see, Emma, once again, I came up against a brick wall and decided to study and find a way to break through. I invented the first compiler. This led me to create COBOL, the first universal computer language."

Grace looked at the large row of computer cabinets and back at Emma, "The navy asked me to return to service in 1967. Even after I retired as the oldest person on active duty, just shy of my eightieth birthday, I still lectured and consulted. I retired as an admiral in the navy," she smiled. "I'm so glad I didn't quit when I failed my entrance exam into college."

Emma looked at Grace, who suddenly appeared before her in a white hat and black navy uniform with gold buttons. She had four gold stripes on her sleeves. Her face had become wrinkled. Her hair, still pulled back into a bun, now had become white. Grace looked intently at Emma and said, "In 1983, I was promoted to the rank of commodore in the navy. This rank was later renamed rear admiral in 1984. The advancement took place in the White House in the presence of then president Ronald Reagan. I am very proud of my accomplishments in advancing computer programming, but Emma, I am also glad that I was able to teach and encourage young people at the end of my life." Grace reached into her pocket and pulled out an 11.8-inch-long piece of string. She handed it to Emma.

Emma reached out for the string and said, "What is this for?"

Grace replied, "That is the distance that light travels in

one nanosecond. Today's satellite communication uses this kind of technology. I hope you find it as fascinating as I do." Emma held the string in her hand and tried to imagine radio waves and light traveling in a nanosecond, or one-billionth of a second. In Grace's lab, a small alarm clock on top of one of the computer cabinets began to ring. Emma recognized it as the alarm clock that Grace had taken apart as a young girl.

Grace looked over at the clock and then at Emma, "It is time for you to go now. Please come back tomorrow during your lunch break, and I will show you more women in STEM and their contributions to science and medicine. But for now, you must turn the program off and step back out of the VR room. Remember not to let Newton out of Dr. Harris's office."

"Okay, I'll be back tomorrow!" exclaimed Emma. "Thank you, Grace, for what you have shown me today."

"It was my pleasure," smiled Grace.

With that, Emma pressed the button on the side of her headset. The room immediately went to black and Grace disappeared. Emma pulled off the headgear to again find herself standing in the white cube. She walked carefully backward to sit down in the chair and remove the special shoe protectors. She was in awe of what she had learned and of Grace Hopper. She was also beginning to see that she needed to study and not give up in school.

Emma could still see the wrinkled face of Admiral Hopper as she had last appeared in the VR program. She marveled at what an amazing woman she had been. She walked to the VR laboratory door to enter the office of her grandfather, which led back to the main hallway. Newton was barking on the other side, eagerly waiting for her to open the door.

6

Cyberwarfare

As Emma walked back into her grandfather's office, Newton barked playfully and jumped up on her. "You are just too cute," she said as she scratched him behind his ears and patted his back. Newton wagged his tail and barked. "Shh," Emma said in a low tone. "Grandpa will be back to walk you along the river. You have to lie down now and wait for class to be over."

Newton seemed to understand and stood patiently by the door as she opened it to walk back into the hallway. "I'll see you later," she added as she stepped out into the hallway and shut the office door behind her.

The other students were just finishing up in the computer lab, so she waited to rejoin them outside the door next to the 3-D printer. The extruder squeezed out a thin layer of filament as it moved back and forth in jerking motions. "Wow," Emma whispered. "I finally get to see it in action." The printer was mesmerizing. It worked with such speed and precision as it created a plastic part under the extruder. She was intently watching through the glass from the chair next to it when Ryan walked out of the office. "How was the program?" he smiled.

"Oh, it was great!" Emma replied enthusiastically. "I got to meet Grace!"

"Wasn't that amazing? She is a copy of the advanced prototype operating system your grandfather helped to create. When he retired, they gave him a copy of all the equipment for his laboratory so that he could keep working at his own pace and develop programs for educational use," Ryan said. "I think he wrote that program first to help girls your age become more interested in STEAM and meet female inventors who could serve as role models. Grace has many more programs to show you. Dr. Harris just finished one about some women at the base. You can observe them with Grace through the VR glasses and see what kind of work they do."

Just then, the first group of students lined up inside the computer lab. "You can join back up with your class, Emma. You are done with your training for the day. Your mother went with the professor to meet someone for a while, so Nicole and I will drive you home at the end of the day."

"Mom left with Grandpa?"

"Yes, something came up while you were in the middle of your program, and they asked us to take you home," added Ryan.

"What about Max?" Emma asked.

"We will pick him up downstairs on the way out. He's fine. I checked up on him a minute ago, and he's having a blast." The line of students began walking by, and

Emma spotted Shania toward the back. Shania waved and motioned for Emma to get in line in front of her.

"Okay, thanks, Ryan, I'll come back at the end of the lecture," Emma replied as she waved back at Shania.

"We will be here waiting on you," he said, with a look of concern that seemed weird. As Emma joined the line, she couldn't help but feel that something was wrong. Why would Mom and Grandpa leave her and Max like this? It seemed odd. She couldn't imagine what they had to do that was that important.

The thought left her as Shania whispered behind her, "I'm glad you are back. Let's sit together in the lecture." Emma pushed her uneasiness aside as she fell back into step with the line and followed the class down the stairs to the second-floor lecture room. She took a seat in the second row near the center, next to Shania. Nicole had led the group, which consisted of three classes and two other STEAM teachers. All of the students, who had been rotating among all of the classrooms, were now in this large lecture room.

Ryan must have taken the stairwell near Grandpa's office, because he had beaten them downstairs and was talking to the guest speaker when she and Shania entered the room. The guest was dressed in a blue US Air Force uniform and stood at the front of the lecture room. Ryan replaced the batteries in his computer clicker, which the guest speaker would use for his presentation. It seemed as if the two knew each other as they chatted together. Shania leaned over and asked, "How was your visit with your grandfather?"

"It was great. He showed me some of his virtual reality equipment and a program he made. How was the computer class?" Emma replied.

"It was really fun! We moved a satellite around space and

added color to the background and to the satellite. We were able to choose different types of attachments for the satellite, and we learned how to rotate it on the screen," replied Shania. "Hey," she continued as she pulled out a slip of paper from her small purse, "here is my phone number and address. I would really like for you to come over to visit and meet my mom. I'm sure she knows who your grandfather is, and it would be fun to hang out, since you don't know many people yet. Call me when you get home, okay?"

"Okay," smiled Emma as she reached for the note. Just then, Ryan did the special clap to get all the students quiet and get their full attention.

"I hope you all have enjoyed your visit to the STEAM Academy today. We always like to end the day with a guest speaker who can explain the new, important careers that will need to be filled in the coming years. Today, we are going to focus on cybersecurity. I have invited Colonel Frank Wayman to speak to you today. He is in the United States Air Force and works as a network engineer. He has also been to many middle school classes to teach cyberskills to students your age. Some of you here today may be our country's next cybersecurity specialists. Let's give him a full STEAM of applause and welcome him to our school." As Ryan walked backward toward the door, he applauded with the students in anticipation of the lecture.

"Wow! That was quite a welcome," smiled Colonel Wayman. "As Ryan said, I work for the United States Air Force as a network engineer. My job is to make sure that the bad guys aren't hacking into our systems and stealing important information or, worse yet, creating havoc with life-threatening results.

"Let me give you an example of the kind of work that my team has done. Recently, we finished a project for which we installed the required classified networks in a new building. We examined the architecture and ran cable from where someone plugs their computer in the wall to where it connects in the communication room, which is where the switches and routers are located. Having this network allows the people in that building to access classified data that can't be listened to or stolen.

"Let me ask you this. How many of you have ever heard of the term 'cybersecurity'?"

Someone raised their hand in the front row and was called on by Colonel Wayman. Emma heard Steven's voice.

"Cybersecurity makes sure that people don't tamper with voting machines and prevents identity theft," stated Steven confidently.

Emma looked over at him at the end of the row, and he glanced over at her as she quickly looked away.

"Good answer," replied Colonel Wayman. "Those are some of the cyberthreats that you may have heard about on the news, but there are many more ways that cybercriminals can harm us.

"Let me give you a brief description of an application of cybersecurity. Let's say that you are playing a game on your computer, and you download the latest modification. You may have unknowingly downloaded a virus, malware, or Trojan horse. I think many of you may know what a virus is, but let me explain how dangerous a Trojan horse program can be. A Trojan horse is a backdoor program that, once loaded, stays in the background of your computer, leaving a door open for a hacker to come in, look around, and find information. Now, being in middle school, you may not have any credit card numbers or information online, but you opened the door for a thief to come in and have access to your parents' information, bank numbers, credit cards, and, worse yet, identification that could allow them to steal your parents' identities."

At this, Emma and Shania looked at each other wide eyed, wondering if they may have downloaded a Trojan horse unknowingly and given a backdoor to their parents' computers. Shania whispered, "That's scary." Emma nodded her head and turned back to hear Colonel Wayman.

"Let me explain it this way," he continued. "There are three different degrees of hacking. We refer to them as the 'white hat,' the 'gray hat,' and the 'black hat.' Now, just like in the old cowboy movies, the white hats are the good guys who are trying to stop the black hats.

"A gray hat hacker exploits a security weakness in a computer system or product in order to bring the weakness to the attention of the owners. Unlike a black hat, a gray hat acts without malicious intent. The goal of a gray hat is to improve system and network security.

"Black hats are obviously the bad guys wanting to exploit information to make a profit. The data is not their data, and they are trying to steal it.

"Okay, now the term 'hack' means to take a piece of software and modify it for another purpose. It may have been designed for one set of purposes, and someone comes in behind the designers and reengineers it for another purpose.

"A white hat is someone hired by the government or a company to find faults in a network before a bad guy can come in and take over the software. The white hat then tells the people they are working for what the problems are and how to fix them.

"Okay, now let me take you to a cyberthreat on a bigger scale. I don't want to scare you, but I have a series of 'what if' questions that I hope will help you to understand how important network engineering and cybersecurity is." Colonel Wayman paused briefly for effect as he looked around the room at the students. Ryan turned off the lights as Colonel Wayman pointed at the whiteboard with his clicker. Immediately, a PowerPoint opened up. It was titled, "What If . . ." He began to show photos of each example as he walked the students through all the ways that hackers could do damage.

"What if someone could hack into the power support of a water purification facility? What if they could mix up the chemical process by switching around commands or shutting down processes? What would happen to the water we rely on every day to drink?

"Or what if they took control of an electrical grid and could shut off supply to traffic lights? It would wreak havoc on the traffic flow in large cities.

"What about patients in the middle of surgeries?

"Are you beginning to imagine all the ways that a cybercriminal could hack into systems to hurt people or to profit from stealing information?

"Let's take it up a notch in devastation. What if they hacked into a nuclear facility and shut down cooling systems and connections to backup generators? The core would heat up and melt and cause radiation poisoning, similar to what happened in Russia in 1986.

"Now let's look at what could happen in the military. What if a foreign enemy could hack into the codes needed to redirect drones or confuse communication among our troops? The people who keep our drone intelligence safe from the enemy are very important to our country. The codes they have are some that hackers and our enemies would pay dearly to obtain."

Emma's thoughts went to her dad in Somalia. She knew he operated drones and also worked on keeping intelligence safe from the enemy. She had a sick feeling in her stomach and put her head in her hands as she shut her eyes.

"Are you okay?" whispered Shania.

"Yeah, I was just thinking about my dad."

The lights came back on. Colonel Wayman put down the clicker and faced the students. "I am here today to help you understand what network engineering is and maybe help some of you who are really interested in math to think about a career in cybersecurity. The United States Air Force has started a program to help middle school students learn about computer skills through a series of games and competitions. I am going to give Ryan some handouts from local libraries that are starting a team this summer. If you are interested, have your parent email me, and I will get back to them with more information for you. If you have any interest at all, think about checking it out this summer.

"You know, in some communist countries like Russia, children as young as eight years old get involved in learning skills once they have taken an aptitude test and score high in math and computer skills. Think about that, boys and girls. They plug them into cybertraining at such an early age specifically so that in the coming years, they can perform cyberwarfare that could affect our country or other nations in conflict with their home country. Not too long ago, Russia shut down the power grid of Ukraine during a conflict. This is just the tip of the iceberg of what is to come.

"Now, I hope I haven't scared you too much. Remember, there are many white hats out there keeping our country safe, but we need reinforcements. Hopefully, someday, some of you will fill my shoes."

With that, he looked at Ryan and smiled. Ryan immediately walked to the front of the room and said, "Wasn't that interesting? Let's give Colonel Wayman a hand for such a wonderful presentation for you today!" In the midst of the applause, the STEAM teachers came in and motioned for their classes to stand and follow them back to their homerooms upstairs to get their things and catch the bus back to the YMCA.

Emma looked at Shania and said with a smile, "I'm really glad I met you. I'll call you later this week and ask my mom if we can get together."

"That would be great!" responded Shania. "See you later!" she said and gave Emma a quick hug before heading out the door to follow her class back upstairs.

Emma took a seat near Ryan and Colonel Wayman before Ryan noticed her and said, "Emma, would you mind going upstairs to the office to tell Nicole we are finished? I will meet both of you and Max in the lobby as soon as I secure the second floor."

Emma nodded and walked toward the stairwell under the Office Use Only sign to go back upstairs. As she slowly climbed the stairs, her thoughts began to swirl around all the information she had heard today. She felt as though she had experienced that feeling that Nicole had described of seeing a light turn on in a once dark room. She had been introduced to amazing phenomena, from the electromagnetic spectrum—where light and color resides—to electrical impulses moving in wires to create backdoors and computer hacking warfare between nations. She could understand how Grandpa had spent his entire life learning more about these things and the unified field that holds it all together. It was all truly amazing.

"The electromagnetic spectrum," Emma said out loud as she climbed the last flight of stairs with her hand on the old wooden handrail. "I actually know what it is! I wish Dad were here, so I could tell him about it. He would be so happy for me."

When she opened the third-floor door, she saw Nicole holding Newton outside the STEAM office door. She was waving his paw goodbye to the students as they exited the classrooms and headed toward the stairs. Emma giggled at his tongue hanging out to the side as students filed past waving and patting him on his head. The hallway was loud and crowded, but she heard her name yelled from the far end and saw Shania wave with a hand motion that meant "Call me." Emma waved back, gave her the "OK" signal, and smiled at the noisy crowd with their lunch boxes in hand and lanyards around their necks. It had been such a fun day!

Nicole put Newton down and attached his leash. She looked up at Emma and asked, "How was your first day?"

"It was great!" replied Emma enthusiastically. "I learned so much in just one day! I think I have had one of those light bulb moments you explained to Mom and me this morning."

"I'm so glad," responded Nicole. "You have no idea how this experience will affect your life decisions for a career and your ability to comprehend your science curriculum this year at school. I think you will see an increase in your test scores!" she smiled. Nicole handed Emma Newton's leash and said, "I'm going to lock up here. Could you take Newton outside to relieve himself before we all get into Ryan's car?"

"Okay," replied Emma, "but how will I get through all that crowd out front?"

"You don't have to go out front," she replied. "There is a side door in the VR Lab that opens to concrete steps. Those will take you down to the second-floor patio. From there, you can take the steps to Newton's private, fenced-in yard. You can't miss it. He even has his own little dog house with his name on it," she chuckled.

Emma laughed as she looked down at Newton wagging his tail. "Okay, let's go, Newton." Emma led him to Grandpa's office. Once inside, she glanced quickly up at Grandma's painting. It seemed especially brilliant today, with the sun streaming in through the window. Newton trotted past Grandpa's desk to the VR door, as if this were his familiar routine. Emma opened the door and again looked at the VR cube where she had met Grace Hopper that day. She was filled with joy for all that she had been given and for the care and concern of the people she had met. She loved this place already!

Newton jumped on the outside door as Emma unlocked the dead bolt and opened it to the concrete staircase that led to the patio. The view was so pretty and featured the city skyline on the other side of the river. The water flowed slowly by, the sun sparkling off of it.

Emma wondered how many times Katharine Wright had looked out her classroom over this same scene during her school day. It was so cool to think that the Wright brothers may have attended a high school play that Katharine had worked on with her students or some other school event. If Katharine had been involved in plays like her English teachers back in Arizona were, Orville and Wilbur must have visited.

The concrete steps had crumbled spots, so she walked slowly down each one with Newton until he made it to his fenced-in, grassy yard. She took him off his leash, and he began sniffing and exploring the perimeter, as if to make sure no intruders had been there.

Emma looked into the sky at two jets on the horizon. She was in awe at the realization that she was in the same city where two brothers designed and created the first airplane with controlled flight: Dayton, Ohio. Mom had said that the Wright family had lived nearby in a small house with their father. The brothers had owned and operated a bicycle repair shop and worked on their flying machine, while Katharine had worked at the school as a teacher.

The jets flew over in formation toward Wright-Patterson Air Force Base. "Now they are everywhere," she said softly. She walked over and reattached Newton's leash when she was sure he was finished with his business and scratched his head. “Come on, boy. It’s time for us to go in.”

She clicked the fence gate behind her and started climbing the stairs. She looked up at the third-floor laboratory door. She noticed for the first time the extra two windows to the left of the VR door and wondered what was in there. Upon entering the lab door and making sure the dead bolt was locked, she noticed for the first time a wooden door in the back of the room. She led Newton over and tried the door, but it was locked. There was a keypad to the left of the entrance. Newton jumped up on the door as if he were used to entering. “It must be a storage closet,” she said softly, “but why the special lock? What’s in there, Newton?” He jumped down, wagged his tail, and barked at her as if he were waiting to go in. “Come on. Let’s go.”

Emma led Newton back into Grandpa’s office and made sure to shut all the doors behind her. Nicole met her in the hallway and said, “Did you lock and shut all the doors?”

“Yes,” replied Emma, “and I locked the dead bolt on the outside door.”

“Great! We’re ready to go. Ryan is in the lobby with Max. They locked up all the first- and second-floor rooms.” Emma and Nicole walked down the quiet hallway to the exit door, which had, only moments ago, been loud and filled with students. Nicole switched off the lights, leaving only the red Exit sign light on.

They walked down the wooden staircase and saw Ryan and Max at the entrance counter. Max had on his backpack and was holding his lunch box while intently telling Ryan everything he did that day. He paused only when he saw Emma walk up with Newton on a leash. He handed his lunch box to Ryan and ran over to greet them.

7

Abducted

The car ride home was filled with never-ending details from Max about what an ecosystem with rivers and swamps was like. He especially liked learning about alligators and told Emma, Nicole, and Ryan about the alligator he put together. It had a sensor in its mouth. “It would open and close its mouth when you waved anything in front of it,” said Max excitedly, “and I made it open really quickly. It was really fun to do!”

Emma sat in the back seat with Max and held Newton in her lap. She chuckled at her little brother and scratched Newton’s ears. She reflected on what a great day it had been and the new friend whom she had met, Shania. She steadied Newton as he jumped up to look out the window. She wondered if he was looking for Grandpa.

Ryan drove and Nicole sat in the passenger seat. They

prodded Max for details, filling in the words of things he couldn't recall. They were both such good teachers with an obvious love for children. Emma still secretly hoped that they might start dating or that maybe they already were. She really liked both of them.

The chatter stopped as they pulled in front of her house. She saw her mom's car and Grandpa's, but she saw another car in the driveway that she didn't recognize. As Ryan and Nicole got out and waited for Emma and Max to get out, she noticed the somber expressions on their faces. Emma again felt that uneasy feeling that something was wrong. Ryan wore the same look he had given her in the hallway outside of the STEAM office, when he told her that Grandpa and her mom had left early.

The front door of the house opened to show Grandpa's tall frame. Max bolted to the door to give him a quick hug before disappearing into the house. Emma followed Ryan and Nicole, with Newton on his leash. "Thank you both for bringing them home," said Grandpa. He looked at Emma and said, "Honey, there are some people here to talk to you and your mother."

Emma handed Newton's leash to Grandpa and walked into the living room, where she saw Father Tom and an officer in a blue US Air Force service dress uniform sitting in chairs across from her mother, who was on the couch. Nicole and Ryan were in the hallway, and Max was standing in front of her mother telling her about his day, oblivious to her swollen eyes, which Emma saw as a sign she had been crying. Mom listened intently, grabbed him, and held him tight as she shut her eyes. She said, "I'm so proud of you, sweetie."

"Ryan, could you and Nicole take Max and Newton upstairs? Max, why don't you show them your collections?" asked Grandpa.

"Yes, of course," replied Ryan. "Come on, Max. Would you like to show us your room?"

"Yes, follow me!" burst Max as he ran out of the room and up the stairs, with Newton running beside him.

"Emma, please sit here by me on the couch," said Sarah. Emma obediently sat down next to her mother and looked at her for any clue to what was going on. Her mother reached for Emma's hand and clasped it in hers. She then looked up at Grandpa. "Emma, I think you know Father Tom from the deployed families support group on base. This is Colonel Ferguson. She is the base commander. They have brought us some information about your dad's whereabouts tonight."

Emma suddenly felt a sense of fear and dread creep up and fill her entire being. She felt as though she were in a strange dream. Her heart began to race as Grandpa nodded for Colonel Ferguson to begin.

"Emma, as you know, your father has been working to stop some bad men in Somalia through drone surveillance. We have received word that terrorists in Somalia have attacked the post where your father was stationed. They seized many computers and classified documents and forced your father to leave with them as a hostage, along with other people from the post."

Father Tom added, "He is alive and well, and for that, we can be thankful. But he is in a serious situation."

Colonel Ferguson nodded and continued, "We are working together with our informants and a Navy SEAL team in that location to find him and bring him home."

Grandpa looked over at her and added, "Sweetheart, we felt you were old enough to know what is going on so that you can be a support and help to your mother as you both get through this."

"We're not going to tell Max," added her mother. Emma looked at her mother, then to Colonel Ferguson. "But why Dad? Why would they take him?"

"Your father works closely with the Combat Communications Group. Their group controls the description algorithms, or radio waves, that are used for target recognition. The military calls this 'IFF,' which stands for 'identification friend or foe.' It is too complex and changes too quickly for our enemies to be able to decipher it. The OSI, or Office of Special Investigations, believes that the terrorists targeted your dad for his knowledge of how the algorithm works.

"We believe there must have been a spy among the contractors who identified David as the lead sensor and network engineer involved in IFF transmissions. The Navy SEALs are a highly trained team that specializes in rescue missions. Fortunately for us, there is a team on the ground there now, and they are mobilizing to find and rescue him. They have narrowed down the area where they think he is being held and have a lock on the perimeter so that no one can enter or leave without them knowing. We know he is alive, and for now, I think it is best to allow them time to apply a strategy to take control of the situation and rescue all the men, including your father."

Emma looked at her mother, whose eyes had again welled up with tears. Emma hugged her mother, squeezed her eyes shut, and began to sob uncontrollably. She felt a hand on her shoulder and looked up to see Father Tom sitting on the couch next to them. "Emma," he began, "we have to have faith and trust that the SEALs will be able to locate your dad. For the Lord knows, right now, exactly where he is, and we know he is alive. The SEALs will find him and bring him home. You need to be brave and do everything you can to help your mother and brother during this difficult time."

Emma looked up at her mother, then back at Father Tom, "Okay, I'm just so scared. I'm afraid I will never see him again."

"The SEALs will find him, Emma," he reassured her. "They will bring him home."

8

Captive in the Enemy Camp

David Harris awoke once more in a chair with his feet and wrists bound. The room was dark, except for a faint light from the opening and shutting of a door down the hallway from where he was being held captive. He could hear sounds of a market that he knew was the Bakara Market in downtown Mogadishu in Somalia. He didn't know what had happened to any of the men in his unit who had been kidnapped with him when the militia stormed the compound. He remembered being led at gunpoint to get in a truck, where his hands and feet were tied. The last thing he remembered was having a pungent handkerchief pressed over his nose and waking up bound and sitting in the chair he was in now.

He hoped and prayed that his men and the civilians

he had come to know were alright and just being held in separate rooms. The only interactions he had were with two men guarding him and working on different shifts. They brought him water, rice and beans, and a crusty piece of bread every day. He always ate as much as he could, because he knew he had to keep his strength up if he were ever going to be able to escape. His thoughts were with his wife, Sarah, and his children, Emma and Max. He wondered how Sarah was managing, as he was sure she must know by now about his kidnapping. He tried to re-create in his mind the last time he was with them. He remembered Max's tears and how he brightened up when David told him he would bring him back a model of the drone that he flew and would teach him to fly along with Emma. He loved them both so much. He knew Max probably did not know the seriousness of his situation, but he was sure that his dad would tell Emma so that she and Sarah could support each other.

Sometimes, in the darkness of his fears, burning tears welled up in his eyes, running down his cheeks. It was during this time that he prayed the most and tried to recall every Bible verse he had ever committed to memory. He had never felt so alone and so vulnerable in his entire life, but he knew that he was probably not going to be executed—or they would have already done it. He assumed he was being held for ransom and would be tortured later as a way to get him to reveal classified information. This is what he feared the most. The possibility of breaking and giving away codes and information that would reveal positions, disrupt communication, and put the lives of the military at risk.

Although it was difficult to sleep, his mind drifted to a memory of sitting on his father's lap when he was a small boy. He remembered when his dad told him that he had to go away for a week and fly to California to meet with engineers. He remembered clutching onto his neck and pleading with him not to leave. He got scared at night when he knew his dad was far away—and what if he didn't come back? His father hugged him and told him to be brave.

This memory was interrupted by the sound of the front door opening. He heard many footsteps entering the room adjacent to the one where he was being held. It sounded to him like at least three men had walked inside, and they began talking in low voices. He strained to look down the hallway through the door, which had been left ajar after his captors had retrieved his plate. One of the men walked into view from the doorway of the room where David was tied to a chair. The man was stout and had a turban on his head. He wore an automatic weapon on a strap across his chest. David wasn't sure, but he resembled the build and height of Mohammed Farrah Aidid, the leader of the militia in Mogadishu and the most powerful of the warlords. He was responsible for seizing international food shipments and used hunger as a weapon against his own people.

Another man entered the room behind Mr. Aidid. He was smoking a cigar and resembled Desmin Atto, the friendly Somalian who often brought them food and supplies from the market. Could it really be him? Could he have been a spy? It made sense to David now. Atto had a pass into the compound and was a trusted supplier of food and information.

Yes, it was all coming back to him. He remembered that the explosion and gunfire began early in the morning, around the time that Atto usually arrived in his truck. David remembered looking out the window by the coffee machine in the kitchen and seeing and hearing guns firing. He ran to his office to retrieve his firearm and unplugged his laptop to hide it. As the commanding officer of his unit, he held all of the classified information and positions of units in Mogadishu, as well as communication codes for northern Africa. He wondered if they had found it. He remembered hiding it in the kitty litter box of the local cat they had adopted. He smiled, thinking that may have been the best place to hide it because he remembered some of the local people's aversion to cleaning a litter box. Actually, the idea came from a story he had read to Emma one night when she was little. He remembered, as they talked about good hiding places for valuables, Emma suggesting that a litter box would be the best place to hide anything from a burglar.

"Please, God, let me return to my family," he said softly, as his head dropped to his chest.

He strained to listen to the conversation of the men but could not make out anything they said. He was learning basic Somali conversational skills to use with local merchants, but these men were talking too fast. Aidid pointed to him, and he tensed as he heard them all walking toward his doorway.

Suddenly, they heard the sound of a chopper overhead. David wondered if those in the chopper were looking for any sign of him or his men. Aidid and Atto gathered their gear, looked out the doorway, and left quickly when the sound had diminished. David dropped his head and waited again in the darkness, with the hope that he would be rescued. He knew that there was a good chance that his situation would be communicated to the Task Force Rangers, who had recently joined the United Nations peacekeepers. They had arrived to try and stop the misery of the Somali people and keep peace in the area. He knew that if anyone could find him and bring him and his men out alive, they could. He just hoped that they would find him before he was taken out of the city. He knew that would be his best chance of survival. There was nothing he could do now but wait and pray.

9

The Wooden Door

Emma returned to the summer camp the next day, along with Max. Her mother dropped them off and went to the base to meet with a support group that Father Tom wanted to introduce to her. Emma had chosen to come to the summer camp instead because she wanted to stay busy and help Nicole. She also couldn't wait to talk to Grace again in the Virtual Reality Lab. She had many questions to ask her about Somalia.

The schedule was the same as the previous day, which meant there was less to do to set up and less of a need for Emma's help. She was secretly relieved, because she just wanted to ask Grace as many questions as she could about Mogadishu and the Navy SEALs.

After Nicole's physics class, Emma collected all the trebuchets and made sure the weights and clay masses were in the right compartments. Nicole directed the students across the hall to the computer lab. Emma quickly wiped down all the tables and safety goggles and checked in with Ryan to see if it was okay if she used the VR Lab to continue the program with Grace. He told her to go ahead as he handed her a small key chain with the keys to Grandpa's office.

"You don't have to worry about Newton today," Ryan said. "Dr. Harris didn't come in today."

"Is Grandpa okay?" responded Emma.

"Yes," Ryan said assuredly. "He was up late, and he just needed some extra time to rest today. This key opens the lab, and the smaller one will unlock the VR room."

"Okay, thanks," said Emma. She reached for the keys and walked toward the office door.

"Emma," said Ryan, "are you all right?"

"Yes," replied Emma, "I felt better after Father Tom and Colonel Ferguson explained everything that's going on. I thought I would ask Grace some questions about Somalia and the Navy SEALs. I can't explain it, but I know that Dad is going to be okay and come home."

"Okay, just checking," said Ryan. "You know that Nicole and I feel like you all are our family too. If you need us for anything, please don't hesitate to ask."

"I know, and thank you. It is so great to be able to be here at the school. I really like it," smiled Emma. She headed toward Grandpa's office, holding the large key between her fingers.

Grandpa's office smelled of lemon spray, as if someone had dusted and cleaned recently. Emma walked across the room to unlock the VR Lab using the smaller key. After opening it, she put the keys in her pocket so that she wouldn't lose them. She sat down on the bench to put on the shoe protectors, when she again noticed the wooden door in the back of the room. "I wonder why there isn't a key to that door." She brushed the thought aside as the excitement of walking back into the computer program began to take hold.

She suddenly had a flashback of arriving at her old friend McKayla's house to ride her horse, Sugar. The anticipation she felt, of seeing the horse and the possibility of riding it, was present when she put on the VR headset and stepped into the cube. The room went black. She pushed the button on the side of her headset. There in front of her was Grace, in the same location and dress in which Emma left her when she stopped the program yesterday.

"Hello, Emma, and welcome back!" said Grace with a warm smile. She wore a white hat, her white hair pulled back in a bun, and she had on her black navy uniform, which had four gold stripes on the sleeves. The sleeves had gold buttons.

"Hello, Grace. Instead of continuing the Women of STEM program that Grandpa made for me, could I ask about some other things?"

"Yes, of course. You have complete access to the program from Professor Harris and can stop and start at any time. You may also ask me other questions—the same way you might research on a computer—if you would like me to explain them to you."

"You mean, I can ask you anything, like in a computer search, and you can explain it in the VR cube?" asked Emma.

"The interactive VR graphics are limited to programs that have been put into 3-D CGI—that is, computer-generated images—but I have an extensive database with the ability to take the most complex information and break it down so you will find it easy to understand. I can also access any image from the internet and can do freestyle comparisons within my data banks, modifying existing VR programs to help you learn visually whenever possible."

"Wow! That's great!" replied Emma. "Would you mind if at some point I brought in a chair to sit down if I get tired of standing? I think I might be here a while."

"Yes, next to the VR door, there is a chair that has 'foot' protectors like you are wearing over your shoes. You may stop at any time and bring it in if you get tired," replied Grace.

"Grace, I would like to ask you a question about this building. Do you have photos of the school and the way it looked when Katharine Wright taught here?"

"I can bring up many photos from the Dayton History Archive and many files on the history of Steele High School and Katharine Wright," replied Grace.

Emma continued, recalling the two windows she noticed yesterday while climbing the outside stairs with Newton. "Where does that wooden door here in the VR Lab lead to? Is it a closet or more of Grandpa's laboratory? Was that Katharine Wright's classroom?"

Grace held a pointer and turned toward a whiteboard that showed the third-floor blueprints of the building. She turned to look at Emma and said, "I cannot tell you what is inside the rooms now, because you are not cleared to access that information, but I can tell you the square footage from the blueprints and how it was used during the time of Steele High School. In fact, those two rooms on the end of the building were, at one time, one classroom, where Katharine Wright taught Latin and English."

"Wow," said Emma. "That is so cool! Is there any way you can re-create the view from her window as it may have looked when she taught here?" asked Emma.

"I cannot give you an exact image, but from the Dayton History Archive, I can bring up photos of the river from this location, looking north." The whiteboard showed image after image of the Dayton skyline and of the Great Miami River. Emma giggled with delight at the photo of Steele High School that had an advertisement for a local bicycle shop painted on the levee wall by the river.

"There we are," shouted Emma as she pointed to the large

Steele High School, Dayton, Ohio (Courtesy of the Dayton Metro Library.)

black-and-white photo. "These windows are where we are standing right now, and these rooms next to us were her classroom! This is so cool!"

Grace ended the presentation by displaying a photo of Katharine beside the Steele High School photo.

"There she is," said Emma. "That was what she looked like when she taught right here on this floor. What a great photo."

Katharine Wright (Courtesy of Special Collections and Archives, Wright State University.)

"Would you like to move on?" asked Grace.

"Yes," Emma replied, "but why can't I know what is inside the room with the wooden door? I would love to go inside and look out her windows."

"You do not have the password needed to access the lock."

"Password? Do you mean a log-in password that Grandpa set up?"

"Yes," replied Grace.

"If I type in the password, could I look inside?" smiled Emma mischievously.

"Yes, I would allow you access, due to the computer back-door privileges Dr. Harris has set up for only you and your voice recognition key."

"Could you give me a forgotten password hint or the number of letters and characters in the password?" asked Emma.

"All I can tell you is that it is a favorite pet's name, a painting, and has thirteen letters."

"Well, the pet is obvious," said Emma. "I will have to think about paintings. I don't know of any famous paintings other than the one Grandma painted for him. Can I think about it and try later?"

"Yes, you may access this VR program at any time. Would you like to ask another question or begin the program?" asked Grace.

"May I ask you a few questions about my dad's location?" said Emma in a subdued tone.

"Yes, you may ask me anything."

"I would like to see where the country of Somalia is and what the city of Mogadishu looks like," said Emma. "That is where my dad is being held hostage." The screen gave a view from space of the continent of Africa and zoomed in to show the Horn of Africa and to the country of Somalia. Grace began describing the time zone and climate, as well as the population and socioeconomic characteristics of the country. She explained the civil wars between warlords and how the United States had intervened to help civilians caught in the middle. She showed Emma photos of trucks bringing in supplies and the endless line of people waiting to receive food. She even showed Emma some of the effects of starvation and what it looked like on the faces of children.

"How awful," Emma said slowly. "I didn't know it was this bad. Can you show me who the Navy SEALs are?"

Grace turned toward the front of the cube and began to discuss how the name originated. "The name 'SEAL' is an acronym for 'Sea, Air and Land' teams." Emma watched a progression of images that started with photos from World War II and progressed quickly to those from the present. "They are trained in special operations in all environments: sea, air, and land. They originated during the Second World War and have become an elite fighting force deployed to any situation that needs a high level of experience and expertise."

"Do you think they could rescue someone in Somalia who has been kidnapped?" asked Emma.

Grace turned to her and told her that the probability of a rescue with their involvement was high. Grace said that the Navy SEALs knew the area of Somalia well, and if her father was still alive, they would find him.

"Thank you, Grace. I think I better get that chair now. I feel a little dizzy."

"I will be here when you return," replied Grace. Emma pushed the button on her headset, and Grace disappeared into the darkness.

"Still alive." The words repeated themselves over and over in her head. What if he wasn't still alive? She felt fear grip her and tighten up her chest. She felt weak and dizzy and needed to sit down. She walked into Grandpa's office, sat down on one of the burgundy leather chairs, and looked up at Grandma's painting. "He's got to be still alive," she said softly. She put her head in her hands and tried hard not to cry. Her eyes were swollen, and she was tired from all of the tears she had cried last night.

With a resolution to be strong, she sat up straight and wiped the tears out of her eyes as she focused on

Grandma's painting. Its swirling colors seemed to take her to another place and time. She imagined flying one of her dad's RCs into a new dimension where there was no worry and everything stayed the same. As she studied the painting and the combination of colors, her mind drifted to the desert scenes in Arizona with the red desert sand and beautiful sunsets. She wondered if Grandma had used some of those colors. She had a few memories of riding out to the desert as a family to look at some of those sunsets and of how Grandma had gotten out of the car to take photos. Emma remembered watching her from her car seat and thought, "It's funny what you can remember from back when you were really little."

She suddenly got an idea. *The Unified Field*! That is the name of the painting in Grandpa's password. Newton must be the pet. Grace said that there were thirteen characters. She remembered how Dad had used the initials of their first names to create a password for their garage door opener back in Arizona. What if the code was NewtonTUF ("TUF" for *The Unified Field*) and *D, S, E,* and *M* (which stood for Dave, Sarah, Emma, and Max)? She said it slowly out loud while counting the number of letters on her fingers. "That works! It's worth a try!" she thought.

She seemed to have renewed energy as she returned to the lab carrying the chair with the padded feet and placed it in the middle of the cube. She pulled down the headset and turned it on.

Grace appeared again. Emma said, "Grace, I think I might know the code. Can I tell it to you now?"

"Yes," replied Grace.

"Is it NewtonTUFDSEM?" Emma looked at Grace and tried to read her expression. It was as if Grace herself was computing and bringing up a program.

"Yes, Emma. That is the code."

"Really?" exclaimed Emma. "I was just guessing!"

Grace smiled at her and said, "If you enter that code on the keypad, you may access 'Skunk work.'"

"Skunk work?" Emma asked.

"Yes, that is what your grandfather has named it. A skunk works project is defined by *The American Heritage Dictionary* as a project developed by a small and loosely structured group of people who research and develop a project primarily for the sake of radical innovation. Since your grandfather was working by himself, he renamed his project 'Skunk work.' The name has been used many times since it was coined during the Second World War by the research and development workers of Lockheed Martin Corporation in California. Would you like more examples of projects for which the term has been used?"

"No," laughed Emma, "that is enough to let me know what Grandpa was thinking.

"Okay, is there any other door I have to open, or is that the only door into Katharine's classroom?"

"That will open the lab and give you access to the transport chamber," replied Grace.

Emma stopped and looked at Grace. Her eyes grew wide. She hesitated as she repeated the term, "Transport chamber? What is that?"

"That is the project your grandfather has been working on for the past seven years. It relays the sequencing of atoms into a molecular string. It works in a similar fashion to a 3-D printer. Layer upon layer of atoms inside DNA strings are unwound and transported through radio waves or photo optic cables and are re-created by a relay receiver on the other end."

"How many DNA strands are in the human body?" asked Emma.

Grace turned toward the whiteboard and a DNA strand

appeared in its coiled shape. "There are approximately thirty-seven trillion cells in your body. Each cell contains forty-six chromosomes, or forty-six DNA molecules. If we were to line up each individual DNA molecule end to end, a single cell would contain an estimated six feet of DNA. If you stretched the DNA in all the cells into a straight line, they would reach over seven hundred forty-four million miles.

"To put it in perspective, the sun is ninety-three million miles away, so this line of cells taken from DNA in your body and placed in a straight line would reach to the sun and back about four times. Dr. Harris unwinds the DNA at a molecular level. That information is recorded in the exact shape and sequence and reattached upon re-entry in the chamber," replied Grace. "In the detached molecular state, any object or person can then be converted into light energy and can travel through fiber-optic cables. It works very similarly to how a computer sends emails across the world."

"So Grandpa takes the DNA apart and can transport it and then reassemble it like a 3-D printer when it returns?" asked Emma.

"Yes, that is a simple and accurate explanation," answered Grace.

"Has he ever sent anything, and did it return safely?" continued Emma.

"Yes, he has sent plants and metal objects and has successfully relayed laboratory animals to a specified electronic address and back with no change or adverse effect on their DNA. His most recent attempt to transport would have been successful if the subject had not jumped off of the fixed point of return and been lost in the field."

"Lost in the field? What does that mean?" asked Emma.

Grace put down her pointer and looked at Emma, "The subject is still alive in the field of electrons that is inside the fiber-optic cable used to transport its DNA. We do not know how long a subject can survive in this state. It has never been tested, but my sensors show that the dog, Newton, is still alive and could be successfully reattached if returned to the transport chamber."

Emma could not believe what she had heard. "His dog, Newton?

"No," cried Emma as she dropped down onto the chair inside the cube. "Why would he send Newton?"

"His journal entry indicates that the seriousness of your father's safety has intensified, as the kidnappers have demanded a ransom and the release of known terrorist leaders who are imprisoned. They released a statement saying that if their demands are not met in forty-eight hours, they will sell your father to another faction that will attempt to extract codes and information from him."

"You mean torture, don't you?" asked Emma softly.

"Yes, I'm afraid that is the pattern that this known terror group takes and has displayed in the past," replied Grace in an unemotional voice.

"But that still doesn't answer the question about why Grandpa would send Newton. Did he write anything in his journal about this?" insisted Emma.

"Yes, his last journal entry was written last night. I will bring it up on the screen so that you can read it." Emma watched as the screen in front of Grace turned into a document with dates. The pages turned and stopped at last night's entry. It read:

June 11

After discussing the seriousness of David's situation with Colonel Ferguson, I have come to the conclusion that I must attempt to travel to the missing laptop and look for clues of where he may have been taken. Colonel Ferguson said that the kidnappers were known to the men in the camp, as there was no forced entry. The explosions did not occur until after the kidnappers were allowed inside. They believe that they were supplying information as trusted informants.

There has been no evidence that they have hacked into David's computer, and it could have information about these local informants that could aid in finding him before the forty-eight-hour deadline. Colonel Ferguson has assured all of us that the ground and air forces are searching diligently. But there has been no movement, and fighting has intensified in the city. To assure his safety, they must find his location and conduct a coordinated rescue.

I performed a test run with Newton in my arms to see if the machine could transport me. Holding Newton has a calming effect on me, and honestly, I was terrified. The transformation went smoothly, as we traveled with the electron orbs to the entrance of the network interface controller (NIC) of Dave's computer, but there seemed to be an anomaly in the field that scared both Newton and myself. I began to experience a tightening in my chest and shoulder pain that I feared was the beginning of a heart attack. Afraid of passing out, I pressed the Return button to come back to the lab, and Newton jumped out of my arms in my weakened state. I fear I have lost my beloved friend, along with my only son. I will try again tomorrow night. This time, I will go to Dave's computer and try to access his files to look for clues. I hope to retrieve something that will help locate him. I will also search for Newton in the field as I return. I have got to try before the forty-eight-hour deadline. I am sure Newton is in the field. I am praying for a safe return for us all. I don't know if my heart will be able to sustain another attempt, but I must try to save my son.

Emma stopped reading and looked over at Grace, "He's going again tonight, isn't he?"

"Yes," replied Grace. "He has set up the machine with the coordinates of your father's laptop email address in Somalia. He will have to bypass the boundary detection devices—such as firewalls and the host-based system security, or HBSS—that prevent hacking and monitor all network traffic. The firewall is used to prevent unnecessary inbound network traffic from accessing the network and computers. The HBSS consists of multiple computer applications that monitor network traffic and detect harmful software. If it finds something harmful on the computer, it will remove the threat. If Dr. Harris is successful, he will have access to all the accounts of suppliers and informants entering the compound. There might be a way to locate the address of the man who entered the base that morning and relay his address to the Navy SEALs."

"But how can he get around the network and access the computer? Won't he be shut down or erased or something if he is caught?"

Grace looked at Emma with the most seriousness and concern that an artificial intelligence could possess and replied, "Emma, if your grandfather is caught, he will be deleted. That means he would cease to exist. There would be nothing to return and put back together in the transport chamber.

"And there is something else, Emma. Dr. Harris has been having chest pains in the past few months. He has taken notes of his doctor visits and recorded the advice given by his doctor to rest. His condition is brought on by stress. There is a high probability that he won't survive a trip through the photo optic cabling. When the molecules are put back together, there is a large amount of stress put on the heart and nervous system."

Emma rested the side of her head in her hand as she leaned on the arm of the chair. She was trying to process all of this. Her dad, now Newton, and possibly her grandfather—she had to do something! Looking up, she cried, "I can't let him do it, Grace. He won't make it! I've got to go instead! You said that the machine was set up and ready. Is there any way I could take you with me, get into Dad's computer, search for the informant's address, and send it to the Navy SEALs?" Emma swallowed hard and felt a deep sense of urgency not only to save her father but also to prevent her grandfather from making the trip himself.

Grace looked at Emma and replied, "I can create any object in the field before you begin. I can attach a receiver from myself to you in the form of a headset. Theoretically, it should be able to transform down to the molecular level with you. I could walk you through how to use avoidance techniques so that you will not be erased and tell you how to search through David's computer to find any addresses or information to help the SEALs.

"We will have to look for a contact at the Pentagon who could relay the information sent to him from your father's computer to the Navy SEALs. I don't think they would act upon a stray email, but they would investigate a tip from the Pentagon." Emma looked at Grace, wishing so much that she was real so that she could hug her, but also glad that she was the amazing computer that she was.

"Well, if I'm going to ride through a field with electrons, and you can create anything for me to travel with, could you please let me ride a horse?"

Grace smiled and replied, "I can create any breed of horse for you. You will feel it and be able to sit on it. But it won't actually be there and will not reappear with you back in the chamber.

"Yes, I can see how it would be comforting not to be alone. Dr. Harris has journaled that the electrons look like flying orbs of light that zip by as if you are swimming in a school of fish.

"Just give me a description of what you would like your horse to look like, and I will create it from my data banks."

Emma shut her eyes and recalled the white drone that flew over their heads when she and her dad flew their RCs. "I want a large white stallion that has a white mane and tail and wings. Can you do that?"

"Yes," replied Grace. "Are you ready to begin?"

"Now? But won't Ryan and Nicole wonder where I am and come looking for me after a while?"

"No, Emma. You will be traveling at the speed of light,

which is approximately 186,282,397 miles per second. You will accomplish your mission and return in almost the same time that you embark on your journey. The time will be delayed slightly in the undersea optic cable. It will be as if you are stopping the program seconds after you begin.

"You have been in Dr. Harris's laboratory for forty-five minutes, and the program you were going to access today would have taken you at least one hour and twenty minutes to complete. There is a high probability that they will not be concerned or even check on you. My sensors show that Ryan is working on next week's calendar, which usually takes him three hours to complete, and Nicole is using the PowerPoint in the computer lab. That presentation has another forty minutes until completion. If we leave now, we will have plenty of time before they notice you are gone."

Emma hesitated and then thought of her dad's face as she kissed and hugged him when he left. She had to do everything she could to help him and to travel through the unified field before Grandpa went tonight. With renewed determination, she looked up and said, "If you are with me, I know I can do it. Let's go, Grace!"

10

Riding with Electrons

Emma still wore the headset but had the visor flipped up over her head. This way, she could still hear Grace talk, even though she was not in the cube and had no VR images to look at. She slowly punched in the code beside the wooden door, saying the letters one by one as she pushed them on the keypad. After she pressed the last letter, she heard the door lock click. She stood for a moment, afraid to push open the door. "Grace, are you still with me?" she asked.

"Yes, Emma, I am monitoring your progress. You need to go inside and locate the transport chamber," replied Grace. Emma pushed open the door slowly, feeling like she really was walking through a hidden wardrobe into a new dimension. She was relieved to see that light streamed in from those wonderful windows that had once belonged to Katharine Wright's classroom. She walked over and looked outside. The river looked pretty, with light glistening off of the water. There were people walking along the bike path. The sky was a brilliant blue. She turned away to look around the room. There was a bookcase filled with books and two lab tables filled with beakers and tubes and a graduated scale.

"Grace, I don't see any kind of transport machine. Do you know where it is in the room?" Emma asked.

"Yes, it is in a room behind the bookcase. If you walk to your right, you will see a narrow gap that opens into a small room. That is where the transport chair is located," replied Grace.

Emma saw the gap, which was about three feet wide, and peaked around the opening. There sat what looked like a pilot's training simulator. It was completely enclosed except for where you entered from the back. There was a padded seat with a computer screen in front and knobs and controls on either side.

"I found it, Grace. What do I do now?" she asked.

"You must enter in from the back and sit in the chair. Strap your shoes into the foot pedals on the floor so that you won't be able to move them. Then place your arms through the openings of the padded circles on the armrests of the chair. They will tighten, much like when a nurse takes your blood pressure."

Emma walked into the back of the simulator and sat down on the chair. She gingerly placed each foot in the pedals, which were secured to the floor, and tightened the straps so that her feet would not move. She then put her arms through the padded circles on the armrest. She felt her breathing becoming more rapid and could feel her heart beating rapidly. "I'm getting scared, Grace."

"Don't be afraid, Emma. Your grandfather has journaled about how painless the transportation process is. You shouldn't feel anything until we are inside the electron flow," Grace assured her. Just think about that white horse I have made for you. He is waiting for you, and I will make sure that the three of us will not lose any connection as we travel to Somalia."

"Okay, I'm ready," Emma replied weakly.

"You should feel the tightening of the armbands, and a cushioned neck brace will rise up from behind your seat. It has a sensor in it to make it stop when it touches your head. Lean your head back on it. This way, your head will remain stationary during the scanning process. I'm turning on the machine now," continued Grace.

Emma heard the machine start with the sound of a low hum. Many lights came on, and some began blinking.

"We will begin the journey on the count of three. Are you feeling okay, Emma?" asked Grace.

"Yes, I'm fine. Please continue," replied Emma.

"Systems are on, and your molecular transformation will begin in three-two-one."

Initially, Emma did not feel anything except for the headrest rising up and gently cradling the back of her skull. Grace continued to explain to Emma what was happening. "You may feel numbness in your extremities, and your vision will become blurry as your DNA patterns are being imprinted and your strings are entering the cabling."

Emma began to feel numbness in her feet and arms, and she had difficulty focusing on the buttons in front of her. She suddenly felt as though she was suspended in a black field and the transport chamber had disappeared. She tried to move and to scream, but she couldn't seem to get anything out. The black field approached a circle that seemed to be filled with brightly colored lights, which appeared to be moving. Once inside the ring of light, she began to breathe heavily and let out high-pitched screams, though the sound was not very loud.

"Emma, are you all right? I am right here with you. You are materializing now within the field of electrons. You should feel yourself riding your horse. Just open your eyes," implored Grace.

Suddenly, the numbness of her arms and legs disappeared, and Emma opened her eyes to see the full, white mane and ears of a horse in front of her. Her feet, which had just moments before been strapped down onto the floor, were now in the stirrups of a saddle strapped to this beautiful creature. She was clutching the horn of the saddle when she saw from her side vision a swoosh of something white. It was the horse's wings! Her horse had wings! Emma began laughing uncontrollably. This was the most amazing experience she had ever had in her life. The horse of her dreams was now a reality—well, sort of a reality. She was riding a horse! A winged horse!

"Do you like Pegasus?" asked Grace.

"I love him!" yelled Emma over the buzzing sound of the lights, which had grown in size and were as big as glass beach balls. Different mysterious lights filled each ball. "What are those?" she yelled to Grace.

"Those are electrons flowing through the fiber-optic transatlantic cabling system that connects internet users between the United States and Europe. We will stay in this transatlantic cable—the TAT-14 cable—connect to France, and be rerouted around Spain and through the Red Sea to Mogadishu in Africa," replied Grace through the headset.

"I've never learned about fiber-optic transatlantic cables. Can you tell me a little about them?" asked Emma as she studied the reflective walls and watched many of the electrons bounce off of the ceiling whenever they flowed over a curve.

"Yes, the simplest explanation is that we are traveling through an optical fiber, which has the thickness of a human hair. This inner core is made up of pure silicon dioxide, and it has a protective covering called the cladding, which helps to prevent light from escaping. The first transatlantic cable was laid in 1956 and was called the TAT-1. It lasted until 1978. Many cables have been put down since then. The TAT-14 was connected in 2001. We will flow through it and follow the ocean floor for 3,500 miles. TAT-14 can carry voices, data, and video information at very high speeds," answered Grace.

Emma listened to all the information that Grace gave her and was amazed at the technology that she wasn't even aware existed. "I thought all of our communication went through satellites. I had no idea that undersea cables even existed."

"Ninety-nine percent of all transoceanic data traffic goes through undersea cables, and that includes internet usage, phone calls, and text messages. This route is also faster than satellite transmissions," replied Grace.

"Emma, we will be reaching our destination soon. You must listen to my instructions and do exactly as I say. There are programs that are in place to stop us from accessing your father's computer. I know how to get around them, but I will need you to listen and relay everything that you see so that I can help you through. Do you understand?"

"Yes," answered Emma, "I will do whatever you tell me to do."

Suddenly, the light narrowed into an opening where the electrons no longer flowed at angles but followed specific paths, making quick turns and stopping and starting. "We are going through the routers and switches, which will take us to the network interface card, or NIC. Once we are binary, we can do anything on the computer," said Grace.

"We will be applying a technique to access your father's

computer that uses a media access control, or MAC, address and internet protocol, or IP, address spoofing. By spoofing the MAC, we will be hiding the identification number of the network interface as well as our location. Once we spoof the MAC address, we can spoof our IP address by building a network packet with a fictitious address. This will help us hide our cyber-identity by imitating another computer. I am applying this strategy now, Emma. This will allow us to be undetected and avoid setting off alarms and firewalls that spot intrusions and illegal entries."

Emma lowered her head so that she could rest her chin on the mane of Pegasus. She knew this was a dangerous situation. She just had to remain calm and trust Grace's cyberskills to gain access. They were motionless now. She could hear computer clicking and electrical impulses respond to everything that Grace was doing.

"Emma, I need you to do a visual scan of all sides while I am working. The computer may have ways to detect us that my sensors do not pick up while I am working. I have hidden us for now, but the firewall is close behind our every move. We will try an avoidance technique that calls for creating a virtual private network, or VPN, tunnel—a virtual private tunnel," stated Grace.

"I'm on it, Grace. I don't see anything unusual, just the same flashing lights in the distance," replied Emma.

"That is a positive report. I am initiating the VPN tunnel. Do not be alarmed by the paths we must take," warned Grace.

Pegasus immediately tucked in his wings and dove straight down, following a series of dimly lit pathways with lights that clicked on and off. The paths reminded Emma of narrow streets and alleyways. Pegasus would quickly turn off one and wait until the next lit path became visible.

"What is happening?" whispered Emma to Grace.

"We are in an encrypted tunnel that will take us straight

to your father's laptop. We will then go through the authentication process, which will allow us to look at his files without being detected. There! We are in, Emma. We don't have much time before the firewall and HBSS figure it out. We must hurry and disconnect the tunnel so that they can't trace us."

"What do you see, Grace? Can you find any invoices from Somali suppliers who delivered anything to Dad?" asked Emma.

"I am scanning his files and have found the name of one person who repeatedly has been paid by the base. Let me cross reference this with any memos or emails from your dad to see if that name appears," replied Grace in a calm tone.

Emma continued to look around the dimly lit alleyway of lights and wires they were hiding in for anything that seemed out of the ordinary. She knew they were in danger, but she was more afraid of being forced to leave before obtaining the information they needed. In the distance, she saw what resembled lightning. It lit up the sky of their location within the network, and something about it did not seem normal. She heard unusual buzzing noises, as if the thunderstorm were sweeping through all the alleyways on the horizon.

"Emma, I think we may have something," said Grace in her usual calm tone. "I have just read an email from your father to his commanding officer. He is suspicious of a certain Somali merchant who has been coming in their gates and suspects that he is working with Mohammed Farrah Aidid. The merchant's name is Desmin Atto, and he has a Mogadishu address on the invoice that he gave to your father for supplies. I have cross referenced invoices from Atto with past delivery dates that show a pattern indicating his likely arrival on the day of the invasion and kidnapping. This is the most likely suspect for the kidnapping, and he could possibly give them a place to begin their search.

"We cannot forward the information directly to the Navy SEALs stationed at the Mogadishu airport. They would not act upon a stray email. The information must come from a trusted person within the Pentagon. I have found the email address of a high-ranking officer within the Pentagon whom your father has contacted often. I am confident that he will forward it to the Navy SEALs commanding officer, since the plea for help and the address where we think he is being held will be coming from your father's personal computer. Would you like me to proceed, Emma?"

"Yes, do it quickly!" insisted Emma. "I see an incoming storm that looks like lightning strikes. It is heading this way."

"The message has been sent, and we will exit the tunnel. Stay close to Pegasus's mane and keep your head low, Emma. I believe we have been detected and are being sought after for deletion. We must move quickly! We must go to radio silence as we escape the network. Do not fear for I am with you," added Grace as the headset went silent.

11

The Mysterious Email

The US Army headquarters and Joint Operations Command were located at the Mogadishu airport in Somalia. The commander of the Task Force Rangers, Maj. Gen. Frank Williams, was surprised to see an email from the army G6 staff (who work in information technology) come to the Pentagon. A cybersecurity specialist had forwarded this email from Colonel Harris. "Something very unusual is going on," he thought. He did not normally get emails from the G6. He picked up his phone and called Lt. Col. Chris Rogers, who was the head of information technology (IT) for the base. "Chris, come to my office right away. You won't believe this, but I've just received an email from HQ G6, who received an email from Colonel Harris. I need to know if this is real."

"I'll be right there, sir," replied Lieutenant Colonel Rogers. Within minutes, he arrived in the commander's office and said, "Sir, I have checked all the systems, and there are no viruses. It is safe to open."

"Okay, let's take a look at it," replied the general as he clicked on the message.

> Please help! I am possibly being held in the home of Desmin Atto.
> 1100 S. Hawlwadig Road
> Civilian Invoice #391
> 05 May

"What do you make of that, lieutenant?" asked Major General Williams.

Lieutenant Colonel Rogers stood behind the shoulder of his general and hesitated before saying, "It looks legit. This definitely came from Dave's computer, and we don't have any evidence that the warlords have gained access to it. It could be from him, sir."

"Well, we've got to check it out," the general responded, while reaching for his phone. "Lieutenant Carter, call a meeting at 14:00 in the hangar. We have a lead, and I need everyone's input." He put down the phone and looked up at Lieutenant Rogers. "Get the team together."

Lieutenant Rogers snapped to attention and replied, "Yes, sir" as he left the office. Major General Williams stared down at the email. "I hope this is you, Dave," he said softly to himself. He opened his filing cabinet and found the file on Desmin Atto. There it was, Invoice #391 from May 5, signed by Colonel Harris. Atto regularly came to their outpost, which oversaw the supply deliveries for the people of Mogadishu. He arrived at the beginning of every month and picked up food while providing information.

All the details fit the time and place of the abduction. There were several Somali militants involved, and all were wearing head coverings to hide their identities on the tape.

He quickly closed his computer, put on his hat, and made his way to the hangar for the meeting. "It's got to be him," he said to himself as he walked onto the tarmac and into the hangar, where several of his officers were seated at a table in front of a large map of Mogadishu.

They all stood at attention. "At ease, gentlemen," he said.

"A few moments ago, we received an email from the laptop of Colonel David Harris. IT has checked it out, and we think it is actually from Colonel Harris himself. He has managed to tell us where he is being held.

"I looked up the Somali civilian who we believe has him in his home. It is Desmin Atto. He posed as a truck driver, delivering food and household supplies, and gave Dave information on Aidid and his plan to attack United Nations deliveries. We have recently become aware of the involvement of Mr. Atto with Aidid and have found that he is one of the top-tier leaders in Aidid's organization. Therefore, we can also assume that Dave and his team are being held for ransom, but the clock is running out, gentlemen. I would like to go in and get him. Lieutenant Colonel Jones is going to lead this mission and assign positions."

Lieutenant Colonel Jones stood up and walked over to the map as General Williams sat down at the end of the table. Jones took out his pointer and began assigning positions, pointing to areas on the map where team members would be assigned.

"At 16:15, forces will infiltrate the home of Atto and retrieve all of our men being held hostage. The Navy SEAL team will go in at 16:16, covering the perimeter around the target area." He stopped and looked around the table. "No one gets in or out.

"Extraction Force," Lieutenant Colonel Jones continued, "three Humvees will drive into the city at 16:17 and hold just short of the hotel here, waiting for the green light once we get the word that Colonel Harris and his men have been found. At the signal, Thomas's group will move to the target and load the captives onto the Humvees. The entire ground force will exit three miles back to base.

"Mission time from incursion to extraction will be no longer than thirty minutes.

"I have requested Blackhawks for air cover and miniguns, and two hundred seventy-five rockets.

"I will coordinate the air mission, and Thomas will coordinate the ground forces.

"The mission launch code word is 'Servo.'

"Questions?" As he looked around the table, no one seemed to have any questions. They had been trained on this type of extraction many times.

Lieutenant Colonel Jones continued, "Once you are in the Bakara Market, you are in a hostile environment. We will be going through friendly neighborhoods before we hit the market.

"Remember the rules of engagement. Let's go get this thing done! Good luck, gentlemen."

The team responded, "Yes, sir!"

Immediately after the meeting, the Humvees and choppers warmed up and men loaded their gear into the vehicles. Major General Williams walked from chopper to chopper and to each Humvee. Leaning in, he looked at all the men and said, "Good luck and be safe." He knew how fast a mission could go wrong. Hundreds of clansmen lived around the alleys and streets of Bakara Market. It seemed that even though they had arrived to help end the Somalis' suffering and starvation, many of the people saw them as an enemy. They could never trust anyone. Just look how Atto had turned out.

The roar of the motors and chopper blades started up. The men triple-checked their gear and rehearsed their roles in the mission. The clock had started, and the mission had begun.

12

Navy SEAL Rescue

Dave Harris awoke once more to the sound of militants entering the adjoining room. It seemed they were getting ready for something. He had heard a car pull up outside of his window before the men had arrived. Would they be moving him tonight? His face was swollen from the beatings he had received. They usually beat him after they brought him food. Some of the militants couldn't understand why they were feeding an American officer when so many of the Somali militants had died fighting them.

Dave braced himself for another assault when Atto walked into the room. Atto pulled up a chair and took a long drag on a half-smoked cigar as he said in broken English, "So Colonel Dave, will you tell us what plans the Americans have for our general before we take you to another camp? If you do, I will make sure your last night with us will be an easy one for you and your men. If not," he paused while inhaling the cigar and blew the smoke in Dave's face, "I will not be able to help you."

Dave raised his head, looked Atto in the eye, and said, "I really can't give you that answer because I have no clue what Major General Williams is planning. Our mission is to keep the food moving to your people. Other than that, your guess is as good as mine."

"You are very foolish, Colonel Dave. You underestimate the extent of Aidid's power in this region. He is a very powerful man. Your forces will never catch him or the people he is connected to. In fact, you are going to be taken out of the city tonight and traded to people who know how to make you talk. I am too much of a gentleman for that sort of thing. I am a businessman," he smiled.

"Are you in business to starve your own people and hurt innocent civilians in your quest for power?" asked Dave.

"I am in business to make money. Those people would die here anyway." With one last drag on his cigar, Atto stood up and said, "Goodbye, Colonel Dave," and walked out of the room.

Meanwhile, the following was transmitted on the Navy SEAL radio call: "Alpha Team in position."

Dave listened as the men talked in the next room. He heard the faint sound of choppers in the distance. Every time he heard them it gave him hope, but he knew that they didn't know where to begin looking. The sound got louder, and he could tell that there were two choppers in the sky. Suddenly, there was the sound of gunshots outside of the building, and he could hear men yelling as several vehicles pulled up. A hail of bullets rang as a battle began outside of Atto's house. Several bullets came through the walls in front of Dave. He rocked over and fell on the floor, hoping to escape more stray bullets that might come into the room.

On the radio call among the SEALs, someone said, "Bravo Team inbound, thirty seconds."

As the Bravo Team secured the perimeter, the Alpha Team ran into the front entrance with guns drawn as they checked the room. Dave yelled, "Over here! Over here!"

On the radio call, someone said, "Charlie Team in position."

Two of the Navy SEALs heard him and ran down the hallway. They found him lying on the floor. David looked up at them and said, "My men—I think they may be upstairs."

One of the SEALs said, "We will find them, sir. Right now, we need to evacuate you." They lifted him up and carried him out of the front door. In a rain of gunfire, both Bravo and Charlie Teams were able to engage the militants and draw fire away from Colonel Harris as they loaded him into the back of the Humvee.

"Stay low, Colonel," one SEAL said. "We have more vehicles rescuing your men at this time. We just need to get out of here to make room for the other Humvees."

Someone said on the radio call, "Cargo recovered."

Another SEAL said, "Charlie Team returning to base with cargo."

Dave could hear from the radio chatter of other units that they were heading back to headquarters as well. All of his men had survived the rescue, thanks to the bravery of the Task Force Rangers.

David smiled weakly and said, "I sure am glad to see you guys."

"We're glad to see you too, sir. If you hadn't sent the Pentagon your location, I don't know if we could have found you as easily," said one of the soldiers.

"My location?" Dave said with a puzzled look on his face.

"Yes, sir, your email that told them where you were being held."

"But I didn't send an email," said Dave.

"Well, someone did, sir, and it was the reason we found you," the soldier said, grinning. "I don't know. Maybe it was some kind of guardian angel or something, but someone was looking out for you. That's a fact."

Tears again welled up in Dave's eyes, and he wiped them quickly away. He seemed to be overwhelmed with emotion from the whole experience and could not stop the emotional release. He dropped his head into his hands as the Humvee approached the Mogadishu airport where their headquarters was located.

"Thank you," he said softly.

13

The Chase

Emma buried her face into the mane of her horse. She could hear the sounds of electricity and see the sweeping search lights of the anti-virus (AV) software. It was using real-time scanning of the internal system to detect, quarantine, and delete unwanted files and programs. She knew that they were one of those files, and she was terrified. Grace was not transmitting to her, and she really didn't know how long they would hide there before trying to get away. With each buzzing sound from a distant alleyway or tunnel, she knew the search was on to find them. She wanted to be back in the fiber-optic cable and away from this computer's "search and destroy" anti-virus program. The rumble and buzzing in the distance sounded like an oncoming thunderstorm, complete with lightning.

After many moments of suspended silence and waiting, she finally heard Grace's voice. "Emma, I have created a Trojan horse program as a distraction. The anti-virus program will immediately detect the Trojan horse and concentrate on scanning and deleting it. Since a Trojan horse is a program within a program, it will take longer for the AV program to scan and isolate it. This should give us time to make our escape. We just need to wait for the right moment to leave our safe spot and run to the network interface controller. Once we are there, we will be transformed back into light and can enter the fiber-optic cable to go back to the laboratory. Try not to be too afraid. Just stay quiet. I think the AV program will take the bait."

"Okay," said Emma quietly. She squeezed her eyes shut and tried to be brave. Suddenly, at the end of the alley, she saw a small movement. She gasped as she strained to see what it was. It was small, with a texture that looked like it did not belong in these metallic paths and alleys. Could it be some kind of scouting software sent ahead to find out where they were hiding?

As she leaned further out over Pegasus's wing to have a clearer view, she heard a small whimper that sounded like Newton when he needed more food or water. Wait, could it be? Yes! It was Newton! "Grace! Grace! I see Newton at the end of the alley. I've got to go and get him," whispered Emma in her excitement.

"Emma, it is almost time for us to make our escape. The chances of you catching Newton and returning in time are very slim. Once we are detected, the computer can find us and erase us easily."

"Oh, Grace," cried Emma. "I've got to get him! I'll be able to make it back."

"Emma, proceed as quietly as you can, so he will not see you and begin barking. As soon as you get him, run back, get on the horse, and bury your head into his mane. If we are spotted, we will have to out-maneuver the electrical impulses to make it back to the NIC. I am not sure what kind of electrical impulses they will send our way."

"Okay," whispered Emma. She slowly climbed down off of Pegasus. He seemed to know what was going on and kneeled down in front, to make it easier for her to reach the ground. When her feet touched the cold, metal ground of the metallic alleyway, she began running as quietly as she could to reach Newton. He was backed into the end of the alley and whimpered with every explosion of electrical energy as the virus detection beam swept back and forth, looking into every possible pathway.

She finally reached him, and when he saw her, he began to bark. Newton ran toward her and jumped into her arms. "Quiet boy," she whispered as she tried to hold his mouth together. He jerked his head free and began barking wildly as she ran back to Pegasus as fast as she could.

Before she reached the kneeling horse, she felt the light beam shine on their location from a distance.

"Hold on to him, Emma. The chase has begun," cautioned Grace.

Pegasus leaped to the air and began following pathways to shake the deleting anti-virus program off of their tail. Emma tightened her grip on Newton and buried her head into the mane of Pegasus as they rolled, dived, and climbed faster than any RC she had ever seen her dad fly.

"Grace, are we going to make it? They seem to be gaining on us," cried Emma into the headset.

"Emma, I will disguise us using a technique called Meterpreter."

"What is that?" shrieked Emma, who had her eyes shut as she held on to a trembling Newton.

"Meterpreter can be used to control a target's machine

and can launch a slew of attacks, ranging from key loggers to privilege escalation," replied Grace. Emma looked up and saw the bulk of the search beams scan and turn toward other lights and electrical movements that Grace had set in motion. Most of the search had broken off to chase other targets, but there was still an anti-virus program chasing them.

"Can you see the fiber-optic portal on the other side of the network interface controller?" asked Grace.

"Yes," replied Emma.

"That is where we need to go. They will see our escape attempt once we head for the NIC, but I have a plan to distract them. You have to trust me, Emma, and do what I say," said Grace.

"Yes, anything!" cried Emma.

"You have to climb on top of the back of Pegasus, and when he positions you in front of the NIC entrance, you must jump toward the opening. It will pull you both in and emit you back out as light. Meanwhile, Pegasus will distract the beam and lead them away from you," said Grace.

"You mean Pegasus will be killed?" cried Emma.

"No dear. Pegasus is a computer program. He will not die. He won't feel anything. This will give you and Newton the time you need to make it to the NIC. Emma, you must do this if you want to survive," said Grace in the sternest voice Emma had ever heard her use.

"Okay, I've got him. Just tell me when to jump," cried Emma.

Pegasus made a large swirl in the air, sort of like one of Dad's split-s maneuvers with the RC. Emma felt the heat from the light beam, and the hair on her neck began to stand up as static electricity was directed at them.

"Ready. Jump now, Emma. Jump!" yelled Grace.

Emma shut her eyes and held Newton tight as she jumped toward the NIC entrance. She felt a pull as she drifted toward the opening. When glancing back, she saw the light beam engulf Pegasus as he led it away from her and Newton. He still dived and circled, but the remaining anti-virus program illuminated him. In an instant, he crackled and disappeared completely.

"Oh," cried Emma. "He's gone. Grace, are you still there?"

There was a moment of silence over the headset before she heard the familiar voice. "Yes, Emma, I am still with you. We should be transformed back into light at any moment and enter the fiber-optic cable."

The dark, metallic grid patterns of the computer gave way to the circle of light with the electronic orbs of color. The orbs grew and began to swim past her as if they were schools of fish. She held tightly onto Newton as he tried to jump out of her arms and chase the spheres as they buzzed by. He panted and barked in all the excitement. Emma held him tightly to her. She seemed to flow through the air as if she were wearing a life jacket and riding a current downriver.

"Oh, Grace," Emma cried, "will I ever see Pegasus again? He was so beautiful and such a wonderful horse. I feel so bad that I caused him to be deleted like that."

"Oh my dear. Actually, he was not deleted completely. I have him saved in my data banks."

With that, Emma found herself staring into the long white mane of Pegasus's head once again.

"He's back!" exclaimed Emma! "Oh, thank you! I'm so glad to be able to ride him again and rest Newton on the saddle. Thank you, Grace!" She kept a secure hold on Newton while trying to memorize every feature of Pegasus. He was so much bigger than McKayla's horse back in Arizona. His large, white wings had beautiful, iridescent feathers that reflected all the colors in the electrons as they buzzed past. "Grace, will I remember everything we have done today?" asked Emma.

"Yes, Emma, you will remember, and I hope you have

learned much about fiber-optic cables and how we used avoidance strategies while inside the computer. You have displayed great courage during our journey today. I look forward to many more days of discussion and discovery as you learn about the world around you.

"Our adventure has come to an end, and Ryan and Nicole are still busy at their computers. You will re-enter the transport chamber in three seconds," said Grace. "Newton will be transformed with his stored program and will be in your lap when you awaken. It is time to begin. Three-two-one."

Emma felt as if she were blacking out and lost all feeling in her arms and legs. She couldn't see anything except the black circle that had engulfed her at the end of the fiber-optic cable. Her thoughts were still vivid. She saw Pegasus, Newton, her dad's face the day he left for his deployment, and the colorful orbs of light that flew by in the optic cabling.

Emma slowly opened her eyes to see Newton still in her arms. "We made it back, boy!" she said wearily.

The headrest receded, and her armbands opened up. As she unbuckled her foot straps, Newton jumped off of her lap and ran out of the laboratory.

She quickly followed as she heard Grandpa opening his office door. Emma stopped in the doorway as she watched Newton bark and jump up on him. He leaned over to pet him and began to say his name with amazement as he reached down to pick him up.

Startled to see Emma, he began, bewildered, "Emma, how . . . where did you find him? I came to tell you that the Navy SEALs have located your dad and are going to rescue him."

He put Newton down and walked over to her. She looked up at him and said, "It was Grace, Grandpa. She showed me how to go through the unified field to search Dad's computer, and she sent the Pentagon an email. I didn't want you to go, because I was afraid you would have a heart attack."

Grandpa held onto her hand as he sat down in his large, green office chair. “You used the transport chair?”

“Yes, Grandpa, please don’t be mad at me. I didn’t want to lose you and Dad. I had to do something.”

“Oh, honey, I could never be mad at you.” He hugged her as he fought back tears. “I’m so glad you made it back safely.”

Emma could feel her own tears welling up as she hugged him once again and looked up at her grandmother’s painting over his desk. The afternoon sun was streaming in through the office window, which seemed to make the swirls of paint even more brilliant and alive with color.

Epilogue

We hope you enjoyed Emma's adventures through the cyberworld! We also hope that you'll join us for future fun adventures with Emma and Newton.

If you were fascinated by Emma's adventure through cyberspace, we encourage you to dive into understanding a little more about the career options available to you in the cyberprofessions. All technologies discussed in the book are real. The only fantasy is when Emma travels through the unified field at a molecular level. Traveling at the molecular level is not yet a possibility in this century! There are many different choices of cybercareers, and just about all of them are growing rapidly. The largest area of growth is in cybersecurity.

From computer technology to business, there are many different cyberjob roles and multiple career pathways. There are two large groups of jobs to explore:

> Computer support specialist: This kind of job requires a post–high school certificate or an associate's degree (a two-year, post–high school degree).
>
> Information technology specialist: This category includes jobs as a computer programmer, software developer, and various other IT careers that usually require a bachelor's or more advanced degree. (A bachelor's is a four-year, post–high school degree).

Here are general descriptions of these two different areas, which have multiple subspecialties:

Computer Support Specialist

Computer support specialists work on many different types of information technology needs. They work with developers, analysts, administrators, and everyone using a computer in an organization. Also in this category are help-desk technicians, who assist those who need help with their computers. The typical daily tasks of a computer support specialist include the following:

- Taking care of network systems.
- Conducting maintenance of systems.
- Diagnosing problems with systems.
- Working with computer users to determine their needs.
- Explaining computer programs to users.
- Installing software and maintaining equipment.
- Helping users with new software.

Information Technology Specialist

This category of jobs has multiple options:

Computer programmers: Programmers learn multiple computer languages when they are studying to earn a bachelor's degree. Computer languages change regularly, so programmers are continually learning to keep their skills current.

Computer analyst: A computer analyst is always investigating their company's current computer system needs based on the business's focus. Based on what they find, the computer analyst then makes recommendations for more effective and efficient computer programs and user guidelines.

Computer systems manager: A computer systems manager oversees the teams running computer programming initiatives within organizations. They also work very closely with the management of the organization to ensure the computer system's priorities help to achieve the organization's priorities.

Database administrator: A database administrator

focuses on software that stores a company's data. They concentrate on the security of their databases.

Information security analyst: A security analyst aims to keep all of a company's systems safe from attack. They are often involved with training the people within the organization, to ensure the safety of its systems.

Network administrator: A network administrator oversees the everyday operations of an organization's computer network. They ensure smooth operation of systems so that everyone in the company can perform their tasks.

If you have an interest in any of these career options, you can ask the guidance counselor at your school about courses you could try in middle school or high school to start building your cybertoolkit. Many schools have computer pathways in which you can start to investigate a computer career.

In addition, there are many great informal learning opportunities that you could try outside of your school. There are several opportunities listed below, and we encourage you to see what options exist where you live. Your local college or university, as well as your YMCA, may have summer programming available that can give you an opportunity to learn more about computers. This list is just a small sampling of opportunities. There are many more, and some are specific to each region of the country:

Air Camp: In this weeklong summer camp adventure in aviation and aeronautics, you'll experience rich and exciting aviation and educational opportunities, such as flying an airplane. Programs are available for elementary and middle-school students and for teachers.

Boy Scouts: The Boy Scouts have multiple programming options for boys of all ages to learn more about computer occupations and skills.

CyberPatriot: This National Youth Cyber Education Program hosts the annual National Youth Cyber Defense Competition. The competition gives middle- and high-school students the role of newly hired IT professionals tasked with managing the network of a small company. In six-hour, timed sessions, teams are tasked with identifying vulnerabilities and hardening the system while maintaining services.

FIRST Programming: For Inspiration and Recognition of Science and Technology (FIRST) provides children of all ages the inspiration to be science and technology leaders and innovators. It engages children in exciting mentor-based programs that build science, engineering, and technology skills that inspire innovation and foster well-rounded life skills.

Girl Scouts: The Girl Scouts have multiple programming options for girls of all ages to learn more about computer occupations and skills.

Girls Who Code: This organization focuses on closing the gender gap in technology. It has programming throughout the United States that includes after-school clubs, summer courses for sixth through twelfth graders on university campuses, and summer immersion programs for tenth through eleventh graders.

NASCO Catalog: The NASCO catalog features multiple educational kits and teaching aids for families and teachers alike.

Space Camp: This is a weeklong summer program that cultivates teamwork, leadership, and decision-making skills through simulated missions. Participants gain personal and professional insights that profoundly impact their futures. Camps are available for those in fourth grade through high school. In addition, there are family and teacher programs.

STARBASE Academy: This is a US Department of Defense–funded program that exposes children to technological environments and positive civilian and military role models found on active, guard, and reserve military bases and installations. The program provides twenty-five hours of exemplary hands-on instruction and activities that meet or exceed the national standards.

Have fun exploring, and we'll see you in the next adventure of Emma and Newton!